# A Girl Called Honey

LAWRENCE BLOCK
DONALD E. WESTLAKE
writing as Sheldon Lord and Alan Marshall

A GIRL CALLED HONEY

LAWRENCE BLOCK & DONALD E. WESTLAKE
writing as Sheldon Lord and Alan Marshall

Cover and Interior Design by QA Productions

A LAWRENCE BLOCK PRODUCTION

# Classic Erotica

---

*21 Gay Street*
*Candy*
*Gigolo Johnny Wells*
*April North*
*Carla*
*A Strange Kind of Love*
*Campus Tramp*
*Community of Women*
*Born to be Bad*
*College for Sinners*
*Of Shame and Joy*
*A Woman Must Love*
*The Adulterers*
*Kept*
*The Twisted Ones*
*High School Sex Club*
*I Sell Love*
*69 Barrow Street*
*Four Lives at the Crossroads*
*Circle of Sinners*
*A Girl Called Honey*
*Sin Hellcat*
*So Willing*

*this is for*
*DON WESTLAKE AND LARRY BLOCK*
*who introduced us*

Classic Erotica #21

# A GIRL CALLED HONEY

Lawrence Block
Donald E. Westlake

# CHAPTER 1

Her name was Honour Mercy Bane and she was thoroughly confused.

She was a very beautiful girl. If she had been in New York, sitting at a table at Twenty-One with a whiskey sour at one elbow and a wealthy escort at the other, she would have been a good deal more beautiful, or at the very least a good deal more spectacular. Beauty, despite the histrionics of a handful of hysterical poets, is more than face and figure, more than eyes and lips and even teeth, more than breasts and thighs and buttocks. Beauty consists also in the trappings of the face and figure.

A well-lipsticked mouth is more attractive than an unlipsticked mouth or, god forbid, a sloppily lipsticked mouth. A well-dressed body is more lovely than a poorly dressed body; unfortunately, the bulk of womanhood being shaped the way it is, a well-dressed body is more lovely than a stark naked body. Just as clothes make the man, the proper clothes make the man want to make the woman.

These fundamental tenets seriously militated against the appearance of Honour Mercy Bane.

For one thing, she was not sitting in Twenty-One. She was standing in the Greyhound Bus Terminal in the town of Newport in the state of Kentucky, and that is a far cry indeed from

Twenty-One. Instead of a whiskey sour at her elbow she had a ratty cardboard suitcase in her hand.

Instead of a glamorous Schiaparelli original, she wore a man's plaid shirt open at the throat and a pair of faded blue denim trousers patched at the knees and worn at the cuffs. Her mouth had no lipstick to brighten it and her hair, instead of being done up in some exotic style or other, was completely uncoiffed. It just hung there.

But she was still a very beautiful girl, and this is striking testimony to the quality of eyes and lips and teeth, of breasts and thighs and buttocks.

Her hair was chestnut. The adjective is currently used to describe any shade that combines elements of red and brown, but in the case of Honour Mercy Bane it was the proper adjective. It was the color of ripe horse-chestnuts with the husk just removed and the nut still moist on the surface, a glowing red-brown that was alive and vibrant in the long hair that flowed freely over sloping shoulders.

Her face was virtually perfect. White and even teeth. A small nose that had the slightest tendency to turn up at the tip. Full lips that were quite red without lipstick. A complexion that was creamily flawless.

Superlatives could also be applied to the body which the man's plaid shirt failed to conceal and which the tight blue jeans made very obvious. Breasts that were large and firm and that got along without benefit of brassiere—which was fortunate because she was not wearing one. Legs that tapered from swollen thighs to properly anemic ankles. A behind that silently screamed for a pinch.

These, then, were the separate components which, taken together, made up the entity known to herself and the world as Honour Mercy Bane. The total effect was enough to bring words of praise to the lips of a Trappist monk. Not even the stain of a tear on one cheek could spoil the effect.

Seeing her there in the Newport terminal of the Greyhound Bus Lines, a passerby might have wondered who she was, what she was doing, where she was headed. Observing her, with the suitcase dangling from her hand like an umbilical cord after a birth, with a lost look on her face and an incongruous set to her jaw, one well might have asked these questions. The answers are simple.

Who was she? Her name was Honour Mercy Bane. She was eighteen years old, the only child of Prudence and Abraham Bane of Coldwater, Kentucky.

What was she doing? Standing, waiting, planning, thinking. Getting her bearings, really.

Where was she headed? She was headed for a small diner at the corner of Third Street and Schwerner Boulevard, a diner called the Third Street Grill.

She was going to get a job in a whorehouse.

Cincinnati is a clean town.

This is an expression and little more. It does not mean that Cincinnati does not have garbage blowing around its precious streets, nor does it mean that Cincinnati juveniles do not write dirty words in lavatories. It means, in the coy jargon of twentieth-century America, that Cincinnati lacks prostitutes, gambling dens, dope parlors, and similar appurtenances of modern living.

The citizens of Cincinnati are no more virtuous than their brothers in Galveston or New York or Cicero or Weehawken or Klamath Falls. They are, on the contrary, as sinful and lowdown and sneaky and sex-crazed and vile as any other collection of people. But, fortunately for them, they have no need for prostitutes or gambling dens or dope parlors. Not in their home town.

They have Newport.

Newport is located directly across the Ohio River from Cincy. A streamlined bridge connects the two cities and makes it possible for Cincinnatians to get from Cincinnati to Newport in very little time. They don't even have to pay a toll.

And Newport, fair city that it is, has everything that Cincinnati lacks. Cathouses by the dozen. Gambling dens by the score, a pusher on every corner, and bootleg whiskey sold over the counter in every drugstore.

Residential Newport is as pleasant a little town as anyone could want to live in. The schools are relatively good. The streets are wide and lined with trees. The cost of living is low; the gambling and whoring and drinking keep down taxes.

Commercial Newport is the living end. No loose women walk the streets—this is strictly forbidden to eliminate amateur competition which would harass houses that charge five to twenty dollars for a quick roll. Dice games can never be found in darkened alleyways; a Cleveland syndicate runs gambling in Newport and runs it with an iron hand. If a person were stupid enough, he could walk the streets from dawn to dusk and from dusk to dawn without seeing anything out of the ordinary. But if he so much as mumbled his wishes to a cabby, he could enjoy any form of gambling, according to Hoyle, or any form of sexual activity, according to Krafft-Ebing.

Newport is a going town.

Madge liked it that way.

She sat at the counter, her big body perched precariously on a stool, her fingers curled around a cup of very light coffee. There was an ashtray next to the cup of coffee and a filter-tip cigarette was burning in the ashtray. A thin column of smoke rose from the cigarette to the ceiling in one long and unbroken line. Madge glanced at the cigarette from time to time but let it burn without touching it. She smoked between two and three packs of cigarettes a day but rarely took more than two puffs from each one.

Madge finished her coffee in a single swallow, then waggled a plump finger at the woman behind the counter. The woman was a beanpole in her forties with stringy washed-out black hair and protruding teeth. Her name was Clara and she had come to Newport years ago to be a whore, failed at it and became a waitress instead. Now she filled the cup half-full of coffee and half-full of milk and gave it back to Madge.

Madge sipped the coffee. She looked as unlike Clara as was humanly possible. Her hair was bleached a raucous blonde, her body as plump as Clara's was thin. She carried a tremendous amount of weight without being genuinely fat, and even though she was pushing fifty she remained sexually desirable, with a pretty kewpie-doll face and breasts that were still mildly appealing although they had lost their pep. Beautiful she wasn't, but she thought contentedly that she could still have a man when the urge hit her without paying some young jerko to satisfy her. If only she could lose about thirty-five pounds . . .

But that, she realized, was out of the question. When you were a junkie who was no longer using junk, you ate. You had to eat or you would get nervous, and it wasn't good to be nervous. Especially when you were a madam. A nervous madam made things hectic for the girls and set the customers on edge, and as a result the customers were occasionally impotent or at the very least enjoyed their turn in the saddle less than they would have otherwise. So you ate—it was better for your health and better for business, and at forty-eight you didn't have to be a beauty queen anyway, so the hell with it.

Madge was a junkie. She hadn't had a shot or a sniff in close to seven years, hadn't touched the stuff since they let her out of the federal hospital at Lexington and told her she was cured. But she was still a junkie and she knew she would be a junkie until she was dead, at which time she would become a dead junkie. She didn't call herself an ex-addict any more than members of Alcoholics Anonymous call themselves ex-alcoholics. She was well aware that at any time she might break down, might take a needle and load it up and pop it into a vein. The physical dependence was mercifully gone but the urge remained. It wasn't a constant thing—for that she thanked God, because if it had been she would never have lasted almost seven years. But there were times when the craving for heroin came to her, times when all she could remember was how good she felt when the white powder had been cooked in a spoon and shot home into her bloodstream.

At those times she had to remind herself of the bad part of it, the times when she couldn't score, the one abortive attempt at cold turkey when she locked herself in a cellar and clawed her own breasts raw when the full force of withdrawal symptoms hit her. And each time she mastered the craving, and now the cravings were fewer and further apart.

Now she was an inactive junkie. She didn't run around anymore, didn't turn a quick trick when the money had run out and she needed a fix, didn't have bad times like when she and Bill and Lucas had broken into that drugstore outside of Xenia up in Ohio to steal morphine, and the cops chased them for ten miles and they threw the stuff out of the windows of the car, and finally the fuzz caught them and she stood on her head in Lexington for a goddamned year . . .

No, now things were a hell of a lot better. Now she had a business of her own, and running a whorehouse was a damned good business to have in a town like Newport. You paid a certain amount every week to the right people, kept a lunch counter in the front of the house so that you didn't look bad from the street, took good care of your girls, talked friendly with your customers, and generally ran a decent establishment. If a girl got sick she went out on her ear. If a girl got knocked up you saw to it that she got rid of her excess baggage in the office of a cooperative and enterprising physician. You made a good living, not enough to get rich on, but enough so that you'd be able to retire before too long, enough so that you ate too much and kept a nice apartment and dressed as well as you wanted to dress.

There were footsteps coming from the rear and Madge turned around slowly. A tall thin man in a tan wind-breaker and Levi's was on his way out and she smiled at him automatically. He didn't smile back and he had a guilty look on his face. Madge wondered idly who he was cheating on—his wife or his girl or his religion.

"Come back and see us," she cooed.

He didn't answer and the screen door banged after he had gone. "Surly son of a bitch," she mumbled to herself, drinking more coffee and motioning to Clara for a hunk of Danish pastry.

Yes, she decided, it was a good life. The house was open from noon to four in the morning, seven days a week, and the girls worked eight-hour shifts. Long hours for whores, she thought, but there was plenty of time when they just sat around on their fannies with nothing to do. Made good money at it, too—half of every trick they turned, as much as they could get anywhere else. But they were worth it, damn it. A girl had to be a Grade-A hustler to get work at the Third Street Grill.

And they were damned good girls. Take the ones she had on the night shift now—Dee and Terri and Joan. She was one girl short ever since that tramp Lottie had run out on her, and the three of them were working like troupers to handle all the trade.

Take Dee, for instance. Dolores was her name, but that was too long a handle to be bothered with. Besides somebody had said that it meant sadness in Spanish and that was a hell of a name for a whore. Now Dee had been with her—she calculated quickly—God, Dee had been working there for a good four years, closer to five maybe. A hustler had to be one hell of a champion to last that long at one place, but as far as Madge was concerned Dee could work there forever.

Dee was tall, close to six feet tall, and she had the build to carry her height. High firm breasts that were about mouth-high for most of the customers. Legs and hips that were damn well

muscled from good honest work. Thick black curly hair and a
mouth that had a fine-looking smile on it even when she was
working away for the fifth guy in an hour. And the men had told
her how good Dee was, how she would do anything and do it
perfectly. Dee was a jewel.

Not only that but the girl was good company. She wasn't so
god-awful dumb like the rest of them. Why, the pair of them
could sit down and talk over coffee, talk about real interesting
things. Dee had been to college for a year; she was no dumbhead
like the rest.

Take Terri, now. Now Terri was stupid, so stupid she didn't
know her ass from her elbow. Fortunately there was another part
of her anatomy which she was able to distinguish from her elbow,
and which she used with remarkable skill. And Terri was easy to
look at, damned easy to look at.

The bell rang and Madge eased herself off the stool and walked
to the door. The man outside was a runt—a sawed-off little pipsqueak with a bald spot on the top of his dumb little head and a
nose that was three sizes too big for him. He looked frightened.

"The counter's closed just now," she said breezily. "Would you
like to go back and see a girl?"

He nodded quickly and she opened the door. He followed
her lead and found his way to the parlor in the back where Dee
and Terri were sitting. Joan was upstairs with one of her regulars.
The sawed-off jerko picked Dee, just like all the little guys always
headed for the biggest gal, and the two of them went upstairs.

Madge sat down again, bit off a hunk of Danish and washed
it down with coffee. Let's see, where was she? Terri—that was it.
Terri was short and blonde, a little on the chunky side but not

so's anybody would mind it. The special thing about Terri was that she made a guy feel as though he was the greatest man in the world. Everybody who had Terri was firmly convinced that he had given her the thrill of a lifetime. This not only made the customers happy, but it brought them back for another go with the little blonde girl.

Joan was newer than the others and Madge hadn't yet decided what was so special about her. She wasn't hard on the eyes, but the little brunette wasn't beautiful by any means. Nothing really special about her, all in all—but she was good at her work and easy to get along with. A good man, according to the song, is hard to find; a good hustler is harder to get hold of.

The man who had been with Joan left smiling. A truck driver who stopped there whenever he had a haul through Newport came in and took Terri upstairs.

Time passed.

Madge was working on a slab of chocolate cake when the bell rang again. She swore under her breath and got up to answer it.

"The counter's closed," she began, then suddenly stopped in amazement.

The person standing at the door was not the general run of customer.

It was a girl with chestnut hair.


Honour Mercy Bane sat with her hands in her lap and looked at her nails. There was bright red polish on them, and she had never had nail polish on before. For that matter, never before had she been wearing such a pretty dress as the red-and-blue frock she had on now, never before had her lips been lipsticked and her cheeks rouged, and never before had she sat in the parlor of a whorehouse at eight-thirty in the evening waiting for a customer.

It hadn't been difficult getting the job. Madge needed a girl, needed one quite desperately with the weekend coming up and the rush sure to be literally backbreaking for Dee and Terri and Joan. Madge's experienced eye quickly knew what Honour Mercy Bane would look like in a dress and what she would look like out of a dress.

Madge had been a little put off at the girl's lack of experience. The madam preferred to hire a girl who had worked at a house before, or at least one who had done a little hustling. This was not the case with Honour Mercy Bane. She had had one and only one lover and that was hardly enough.

But she was beautiful, which made a big difference.

"Crap," Madge had said. "Fust thing we'll have to do is change your name. Can't have a whore named Honour and Mercy. It'd keep the customers from feeling right about the whole thing. Hell, you look too much like a virgin as it is. How do you go for the name Honey?"

Honey was all right with Honour Mercy Bane.

"Straight's ten bucks, half-and-half is fifteen, French is twenty," Madge informed her. "Anything special, you make your own price. You want to cut your rate it's your business, but you pay me half of the asking price, no matter how much you get. And don't think you can hold out on me. You might try to give me ten bucks for a French where you collected twenty and tell me you turned a straight trick. You'll get away with it for a while, but the minute I catch on you go out on your fanny."

"I wouldn't cheat you," said Honour Mercy Bane. And she was telling the truth because she never cheated anyone.

"You'll live in the Casterbridge Hotel down the street," Madge told her. "Gil Gluck runs it and he gives all my girls a straight deal. Ten bucks a week for a private room with private bath and it's a good clean place."

Honour nodded in agreement. She really didn't care where she lived.

"I'm trying you on the night shift this week," Madge went on. "It's probably a mistake, what with you so inexperienced, but I rotate the girls every two weeks and I don't want to mess up the schedule." Honour nodded again.

"Dee's just finishing up," Madge said. "She's been up there with a little pipsqueak of a guy for better'n fifteen minutes. Any second now she'll be down and she'll show you what's what and get some clothes for you and all."

A minute or two later a small man with a bald spot on the top of his head appeared with a huge smile on his face. In another minute a tall girl appeared with a smile on her own face and Madge introduced them. And up the stairs they went.

Dee taught her the ropes. The lesson was a time-consuming one but Dee didn't seem to mind. She taught Honour how to dress, how to undress, how to make up her face, how much perfume to use and where to put it, what to say to the customers, what they would want her to do and how to do it, how to make them want special things and how to do the special things, how to excite an impotent man, and how to make a man get through fast.

Important things.

How to clean herself so that she wouldn't get sick or pregnant. How to freshen up after finishing with one customer so that she would be ready for the next in a matter of seconds. How to be bright and friendly, how to look sexually desirable always.

Honour listened carefully. The tall brunette never had to repeat a word, and Honour remembered every word she was told. She concentrated and learned very quickly.

When the house closed, she went with Dee to the Casterbridge Hotel, a block away on Schwerner Boulevard and Fourth Street. There she was assigned a room on the second floor with a private bathroom and a comfortable bed and a nice rug on the floor. She took a restful bath, unpacked her ratty cardboard suitcase, and went to bed. She fell asleep at once.

The next morning she was awake by ten. It was Friday and she would start work that evening at eight o'clock. She had breakfast at a little restaurant on Fourth Street—Madge had advanced her fifty dollars against future earnings—and then went shopping. She followed Dee's elaborate instructions and bought what clothing she would need for the job, plus what cosmetics and supplies would be necessary.

Now it was 8:30. Dee and Terri and Joan were all upstairs with their first customers of the evening; soon it would be her turn. She sat alone in a lounge chair in the parlor, waiting for her first customer, her hands in her lap and her whole body in perfect repose.

Perhaps you are wondering what she was doing there, getting ready to play the whore in a room above the Third Street Grill in Newport. This was precisely what she was thinking about just then . . .

•          •          •

Fifteen hundred people live in Coldwater, Kentucky. Abraham and Prudence Bane lived in a small white frame house on the outskirts of town. Abraham Bane was a foreman at a distillery which was the town's sole industry; Prudence Bane was a housewife. They were good God-fearing Baptists, both of them, and their household was run according to the tenets of a frightening brand of Puritanism that started with Wycliffe and ran downhill via Cromwell and Cotton Mather until it lay half-buried in the Kentucky foothills.

Abraham and Prudence Bane lived by the Bible. Although Abraham Bane worked at the Kelmscott Sour Mash Distillery and served that distillery with a loyalty second only to the loyalty he bore to his strange and fearful God, not a drop of bourbon had ever passed his lips. He and his wife lived the clean life, the good life, and while their idea of an exciting evening was a hot game of checkers in front of the fireplace, the promise of heaven more than compensated for the relative boredom of their existence.

With this in mind, you may readily understand their violent reaction when they discovered their daughter, Honour Mercy Bane, with a man.

They were appalled.

The man who occupied the place of honor with Honour was a schoolteacher in the Coldwater high school, a thin and nervous man named Lester Balcolm. He had made love to Honour Mercy Bane many times before the two of them had been discovered in the act. He had told her that he loved her, and while she did not believe him, she did know several things. She knew the way her mouth tingled when he kissed her, the way her tongue felt deliciously alive when his tongue touched it and caressed it. And, finally, she knew what it was like to accept his manliness, to move with him and move with her own passion until it happened for both of them and they were bathed in the sweet sweat of love.

But they were discovered. Lester Balcolm left Coldwater with the marks of Abraham Bane's belt on his thin back and the warning that he would be killed if he was ever found in Coldwater again. Honour Mercy Bane left Coldwater with a ratty cardboard suitcase in her hand and the advice never to return ringing in her ears.

"You're no good," they told her. "You're not our daughter any longer."

And so she left.

"Go to Newport," they told her. "Be a bad woman there. You're not our daughter." And so she did.


The man was huge. He had a shock of red hair that stood straight up on his cannonball head and eyes that looked like those of a recently slaughtered hog. He grinned at Honour Mercy Bane and she led him up the winding flight of stairs to the room that was hers for the evening.

They entered the room and she closed the door. She smiled as she had been taught to smile and the man grinned as he had grinned before.

"My name's Honey," she said.

"Good," the man said.

Her smile widened. "How do you want it?"

"What's on the menu?"

She told him the three standard varieties and the price of each. Then he smiled, reached out a hand and gave her breast a pinch. He didn't hurt her but she realized that with his muscles he could probably rip her breast right off her.

"I got a better idea," he said. "I got something special the two of us can do."

# Chapter 2

A man AWOL is a man running scared. Richie Parsons was a man AWOL, and he was scared out of his mind. A boy AWOL, really, for Richie Parsons had crept into his eighteenth year only a scant four months ago.

Richie Parsons was running scared. He was used to being scared, he'd been scared of one thing or another as long as he could remember, but he wasn't used to running. He'd never run before in his life, he'd always crept or sidled or tiptoed. His grammar school teachers had talked about him as "the shy, quiet little boy, the one who always edges along the wall, as though afraid to be seen." His high school teachers had mentioned him as "the loner, the boy who doesn't belong to the group, but only creeps around the fringes, watching and silent." His Tactical Instructor in Air Force boot training had complained about him as "the little sneak with two left feet." His contemporaries, in grammar school and high school and the Air Force, at all times and all ages, had spoken of him as "the gutless wonder."

Richie Parsons, eighteen years old, five foot seven-and-one-half inches tall, weighing one hundred thirty-five pounds, with watery eyes of a washed-out blue and Kansas drought blond hair, was everything everyone had ever said about him. He was silent, solitary, sneaky and gutless. And, at the present moment, he was also running and scared.

He'd hated the Air Force. He'd hated it from the minute he'd walked into the recruiting center for his physical and his qualification tests. He'd been one of a group of about fifty young men, thrown into close proximity with them all, and he'd hated that. When he'd tried to move back against the wall, away from the milling jumble, a uniformed sergeant had hollered at him to get back with the group.

They had all been herded into a long, cold, linoleum-floored room, and they had all had to strip, down to their shoes. Then they were fifty chunks of ill-assorted, poorly developed, goose-bump-covered flesh, forming a long line and shambling on by the bored and annoyed doctors, whose examination might have been funny if it hadn't been so pathetic.

Richie had hoped he would fail the physical. He knew he was weak, he knew he was underweight, and his eyes, without his plastic-rimmed glasses, were almost useless. But every doctor had passed him, even though he had fainted when they took the blood sample from his arm. He had fainted, calling attention to himself, and when he came back to consciousness, lying on the Army cot near the busily stabbing doctor, the rough Army blanket itchy against his nakedness, the whole line was looking at him. Frightened, embarrassed, so nervous he could hardly stand. He had crept back into the line, hoping they would all forget him, look at somebody else for a change, hoping somebody else would faint and draw the crowd's attention away from him.

He had passed the physical. But he still believed there was a chance he would fail the mental tests, the qualification exams.

Until he took them, that is, he believed he might stand a chance of failing them. After all, he had never done very well in school. He had spent seven years getting through the first six grades of grammar school, and four years getting through the three grades of junior high school. He had only gone to senior high school one year, had flunked half the courses, and quit school at seventeen to join the Air Force.

But Mama hadn't wanted him to join the Air Force. Mama hadn't wanted Richie to do anything not suited to a boy of ten. So Richie had to wait until his eighteenth birthday, when he could enlist without Mama's consent.

And already, even before actually enlisting, he hated it, and he hoped he would fail the qualification tests, because he would never have the courage to just turn around and walk out. He would be doing something different, calling attention to himself, and he just couldn't do it.

Nor could he fail the qualification tests. High score was one hundred. Passing score was ten. If Richie Parsons had been imported just that day from the jungles of the upper Amazon, speaking only Ubu-Ubu and unable to read or write, he still could have passed the Armed Forces Qualification Test. In fact, there were three Puerto Ricans among the fifty enlistees, three Puerto Ricans who spoke only Spanish, and *they* passed the test.

The test went like this: On the left is a picture of a screwdriver. On the right are four pictures, a wrench, a hammer, a screwdriver, and a pair of pliers. You have to match the picture on the left with the similar picture on the right. If you make a mistake, one of the recruiters will come to you and "explain the instructions" to you again, to make sure you do it right.

Richie tried to fail. He tried his darnedest to fail, and he got a score of forty-eight. He passed with drooping colors.

In his four-month Air Force career, the only thing Richie really came close to flunking was basic training. Left and right were totally mysterious concepts to him. It took him a month to understand that spitting on a shoe doesn't make it dirty; when done right, spitting on a shoe makes the shoe shinier than ever. During familiarization with the carbine (in which there is no failing score), he plugged virtually every target on the field except his own. He was always at the wrong end of the formation when his group had KP, and he always wound up either in the garbage room or the grease trap. There were seventy-two trainees in his basic training flight, and his Tactical Instructor assured him he was by far the worst of the lot. When they all went to the indoor swimming pool to learn the proper way to jump off a torpedoed ship, in case they ever were onboard a ship and it happened to be torpedoed, Richie Parsons was the only one of the seventy-two basic trainees who had to be dragged, half-drowned, out of the pool.

There is always petty thievery in a barracks containing seventy-two young men. There was petty thievery in Richie Parsons' barracks, too. The petty thief is usually never discovered. Richie Parsons was never discovered either.

Richie Parsons had never once been discovered, in a lifetime of petty thievery. It had begun with Mama's purse, from which an occasional nickel or dime filched wasn't noticed. It had moved on to the grammar school cloakroom, where candy bars and coins, even if their absence were noted, could certainly never be traced. The junior high school locker-room had been next, and the magazine rack at the neighborhood candy store. And in the Air Force it was his barracks-mates' wall– and foot-lockers.

He was never discovered. He was never even suspected. His perfect record of perfect crime was not the result of any brilliant planning on his part at all. He didn't plan a thing. His perfect record was caused by equal parts of his own personality and dumb luck. His own personality, because he was such an *obvious* sneak. No one in the world skulked quite as obviously as Richie Parsons. No one in the world was as obviously incompetent in absolutely everything. A guy who is completely obvious in his sneaking, and completely incompetent in his actions, could never possibly get away with petty thievery. The idea never even occurred to anybody. During the eleven weeks of basic training, almost everybody in the flight was suspected at one time or another, but no one ever suspected clumsy, obvious Richie Parsons.

During the last couple of weeks of basic training, Richie and his fellow-trainees were classified. That is, they were tested, inspected, and assigned their particular Air Force careers, usually on the round-peg-square-hole method. Richie was given an IQ test, and amazed everybody, including himself, by coming up with a score of 134. Apparently, hidden down beneath the layers of confusion and cowardice and inferiority feelings, way down deep inside Richie Parsons, where it was never used, was a mind.

On the basis of this IQ score, and because it was one of the few careers open that week, Richie Parsons was assigned to Personnel Technical School, at Scott Air Force Base, near St. Louis, Missouri. He was given a seven-day leave at home after basic training, where Mama slobbered over him at every opportunity, and he edged along walls more furtively than ever, and then he took the bus and reported to the school squadron at Scott Air Force Base.

The Personnel Technical School was ten weeks long, but Richie Parsons only lasted the first three weeks. Then, all at once, he was AWOL and running scared.

It was the petty thievery again. There were only fifty-six young men in the barracks with Richie at Scott, and the barracks had been given interior partitions, forming cubicles, in each of which slept four men. There were no doors on the cubicles, no way to seal them off from the outside world.

As usual, in an open or semi-open barracks, there was petty thievery. As usual, no one suspected bumbling Richie Parsons, who was having such a terrible time in school, and who still didn't know his left from his right. No one paid much attention to the fact that most of the thievery was done on weekends, when everybody else was in East St. Louis, and Richie Parsons was practically alone in the squadron area.

Richie Parsons went to St. Louis twice, and East St. Louis once. St. Louis and East St. Louis have virtually the same relationship as Cincinnati and Newport. St. Louis is a clean town, where *all* the bars close at midnight, and the local churches have free Sunday breakfasts for the soldier boys from the air base and the Army camps that ring that city. East St. Louis is a hell-hole, where the bars never close, the cathouses have everything but neon signs, and the soldier boys work up their appetites for Sunday morning breakfast across the river.

The first time Richie Parsons went to St. Louis, he attended a major league baseball game, which was free to men in uniform. He'd never seen a major league baseball game, and it disappointed him. The second time, he went to the concert at Kiel Auditorium, which was also free to men in uniform. He'd never been to a concert either, and that bored him stiff.

The one time he went to East St. Louis, he was brought along by a few other guys and he was scared out of his wits. While the other guys trooped into the whorehouse, Richie stayed out on the sidewalk, furtive and scared and lonely, the gutless wonder to the end, incapable of either going inside to lose his virginity or going back to the base to save it. A dark-haired, evil-grinning girl in a ground-floor window of the whorehouse kept talking to him, saying, "Wanna make it with me, airman? We go round the world for fifteen, boy. Come on, live a little. Wanna see what I got for you? Hot stuff, airman. I do anything you want, boy, all you has to do is ask."

Richie made believe he didn't hear the woman, cooing at him from the window. He walked jerkily back and forth in front of the building, head down, staring hopelessly at the sidewalk and wishing he'd stayed at the base or gone to the USO in St. Louis. But all you could do at the USO was dance with high school girls, and he knew he'd be too afraid to ask a strange girl to dance with him. Besides, he was a terrible dancer; he danced the way he walked, furtively, sneaking and shuffling, round-shouldered.

Nobody noticed that the stealing didn't happen when Richie Parsons was in town. But everybody noticed the stealing, and people began to get mad about it. The Captain, the commander of the squadron, heard about it, and he called a special formation of that barracks, because there was more filching than usual going on there. "I want you men to find the sneak-thief in your midst," he told them, passing the buck. "You know the other men in your barracks with you. I want you to find him, and I want you to drag him to my office by the heels. And I won't raise a fuss if you kick his ass before you bring him to me."

Everybody liked that. The Captain was all right. Everybody watched everybody else, and nobody trusted anybody.

But still nobody noticed Richie Parsons.

Until that last Saturday night. A six-foot fullback named Tom Greery decided to find out who the hell the dirty crook was. He didn't go to town that Saturday night, though he would have loved to spend another ten on that red-haired Bobbi in the cathouse on Fourth Street. He stayed in the barracks, lying on the floor under his bed, looking down the row of cubicles at the shoes and bed-legs. The partitions didn't reach all the way to the floor, and he had a clear view all the way to the end of the barracks.

He spent four hours under the bed, impatiently waiting for something to happen. He kept thinking about red-headed Bobbi, with the pneumatic drill hips, and he kept getting madder and more impatient by the minute.

And finally he saw movement. Way down at the other end of the row of cubicles, a pair of feet came into view. They moved around in that cubicle for a minute, and Greery wondered whether he should make his move yet not. But this might not be the sneak-thief. It might be a guy who bunked in that cubicle, and Greery didn't want his presence to be known too early. Not until the lousy bastard son-of-a-bitch of a thief showed up.

The feet, moving very softly, left that first cubicle, and reappeared in the second. Greery watched, growing more and more sure of his quarry. When the feet moved on to the third cubicle, Greery was positive he had his man. Awkwardly, trying to be absolutely silent, he crawled out from under his bed and tiptoed down the center corridor, past the empty and defenseless cubicles, to the one where his man was waiting. He got to the doorway, looked in, and saw Richie Parsons with both hands in Hank Bassler's foot-locker.

"All right, you son-of-a-bitch," said Greery, and Richie leaped around, terror and confusion distorting his face. "Now," said Greery, "I'm going to kick the hell out of you."

"Please," said Richie, but that was all he said. Because Greery was as good as his word. He kicked the hell out of Richie Parsons, and then he dragged him, with a painful grip on Richie's elbow, out of the barracks and down the row to the Squadron Headquarters building.

But the Captain, too, was in East St. Louis, working up an appetite for Sunday morning. There was no one in HQ but the Charge of Quarters, an unhappy airman given the duty of sitting around the orderly room all Saturday night, in case the phone rang.

Greery shook Richie Parsons by the elbow, and announced to the Charge of Quarters, "I got the bastard. The lousy sneak-thief."

"This one?" asked the CQ in surprise.

"Caught him red-handed," said Greery. He spoke in capitals. "Caught Him In The Act!"

"You want me to call the AP's?" asked the CQ.

"No," said Greery, considering. "The Captain will want to see this little son-of-a-bitch." He shook Richie again, and glowered at him. "You hear me, you bastard?" he said. "You are going to go on back to the barracks, and you are going to hit the rack, and you are going to stay there until Monday morning. You hear me?"

Richie nodded, quivering.

"Eight o'clock Monday morning," said Greery, "we are going to go in and see the Captain. You better show up, too. If you don't, you're AWOL. You've got your ass in a sling as it is, so don't add AWOL to everything else."

Richie shook his head, mute and terrified.

Greery dragged the sneak-thief back to the barracks, booted him through the doorway, and went off to town to see the red-head, Bobbi.

Ninety-nine out of a hundred people in Richie Parsons' position would have stayed and taken their punishment. Richie had only been in the Air Force four months, and he had been well-indoctrinated, as all recruits are, in the horrors of going AWOL. It was, all things considered, a much more serious crime than thievery.

Besides, ninety-nine out of a hundred in Richie Parsons' position would have realized they could beat the rap without half trying. Monday morning, you go to see the Captain. You're all bruised up, because Greery kicked the hell out of you. You look scared and remorseful and hang-dog. You throw yourself on the Captain's mercy. You tell him this is the first time you've ever done anything like this, and you don't know what made you think you could get away with it. You mention—not as an excuse, because you know and admit there isn't any excuse for your terrible behavior, but just in passing—you mention the fifty-dollar allotment (out of your eighty-four-dollar a month pay) that you are sending home to your widowed mother. The Captain looks at your Service Record and sees that you do have a fifty-dollar allotment made out to Mama, and that your father is dead. He sees how contrite and terrified you are, and he sees that you've had the crap kicked out of you. So he gives you a stern chewing-out, and lets you go, with the warning that next time you'll be court-martialed. You go back to the barracks, where everybody joins in to kick the crap out of you again, and it's all over and forgotten. And you don't do any more stealing until you've been reassigned somewhere where nobody knows you.

Ninety-nine out of a hundred people could have figured that out, and acted accordingly. Richie Parsons never did go along with the group, not in anything.

Richie Parsons went AWOL.

He packed a small suitcase, stuffing some uniforms and underwear into it, put on civilian slacks and shirt and jacket, and took the base bus to the front gate. East St. Louis was down the road to the left, to the west. Richie headed to the right, to the east.

The only sensible thing he did was bring along a complete uniform. They'd told him in basic training what the difference was between AWOL and Desertion. When you were AWOL, you figured to come back some day. When you Deserted, you planned to never come back. And the evidence that counted was your uniforms. If you threw your uniforms away, or sold them, or pawned them, then you weren't planning to come back. You were a Deserter. If you held on to your uniforms, you were planning to come back. You were only AWOL. The difference being that Deserter gets a Dishonorable Discharge, and somebody who's AWOL gets thirty days in the stockade.

Richie Parsons wasn't planning on coming back to Air Force, not ever. But he remembered the ground rules of the game, so he brought along a complete uniform, just in case he was caught.

He headed east across Illinois, hitchhiking, terrified of cops and Air Police and just about every adult male he saw. He got a few rides, across Illinois and southern Indiana and into Kentucky, and up through the tobacco fields of Kentucky toward the Ohio border and Cincinnati. And one ride he got left him in Newport, Kentucky, at nine o'clock on Monday evening. The old farmer who'd given him the ride pointed out the direction to the bridge for Cincinnati, wished him luck, and putted away down a side street. Richie started walking, lugging his suitcase.

He was running, and he was scared. He didn't know where to go, he didn't know what to do. He knew only that he couldn't go home, to Albany, New York. He knew the Air Police would first look for him there, and they would watch his house. He couldn't go home.

And he didn't know anyone at all anywhere else in the world. Billions and billions of people in the world, and he knew only a handful of them. A few relatives and schoolmates in Albany. A few guys who hated him at Scott Air Force Base. He didn't know anybody at all anywhere else in the whole wide world.

He had about sixty dollars left. He'd gone through the barracks like a vacuum cleaner before he left, grabbing bills, change, rings, watches, electric razors, everything he found that could possibly be turned into cash. He'd had to carry the stuff on him all weekend, but today, Monday, he had pawned his way across Kentucky, leaving one or two pieces of stolen property in every pawnshop he saw. All he had left now were a watch and a high-school ring, and the pawnshops were closed at that hour. They would go tomorrow.

He was hungry. He hadn't eaten since ten o'clock this morning.

He decided to find a diner or something here in Newport, before walking to Cincinnati and hitchhiking farther on to wherever it was he was going.

He was on Third Street, with Schwerner Boulevard just ahead. Down at the corner was a diner, with a modest red neon sign saying, "Third Street Grill."

He walked faster, feeling the hunger pangs inside him. He got to the diner and pushed on the door, but nothing happened. He looked through, and saw that the diner was all lit up. A skinny, stringy woman in a soiled white apron was behind the counter, and a plump, well-girdled, incredibly blonde woman was sitting on one of the stools, drinking coffee and eating Danish pastry.

The place was open. That was obvious. But the door was locked, or stuck, or something. Richie looked at the door, trying to figure out how to open it, and saw the bell-button on the right. He'd never been in Newport before. He'd never been much of anywhere before. As far as he knew, you had to ring the bell to get into all diners in Newport. Maybe that was the way they worked it.

He pushed the button.

The plump woman eased herself off the stool and padded to the door, looking heavy and ominous and much too mother-image. Even before she opened the door, Richie Parsons was terrified, his mind a daze.

The woman opened the door, and grinned at him. "The counter's closed just now," she said, speaking rapidly in an obviously routine pattern. "Would you like to go back and see a girl?"

Richie was a blank. The woman had asked him a question, something that had sailed on over his head. He was afraid she suspected him, that she would turn any second and call the police: "We've got a Deserter here for you!"

He nodded, jerkily, hoping it was the right answer, hoping his face wasn't giving him away, hoping he'd get out of this all right, and be able to hurry on out of Newport.

It was the right answer. The woman's smile broadened, and she stepped back from the doorway, motioning to Richie to come in. He did, and followed her through a door to the right of the counter. She motioned for him to go on back, patted him chummily on the arm, and went away to the front again.

Richie, not knowing what else to do, barely knowing his own name at this point, kept on down the hall, and found himself in a dim-lit parlor, where a girl with reddish-brown hair and a smiling mouth was looking at him from where she sat in an over-stuffed chair near a doorway and a flight of stairs leading up.

The girl got to her feet and walked toward him, smiling, her eyes fastened on his, her body undulating gently as she moved. "Hi," she murmured. "My name's Honey."

And Richie Parsons, numbly gripping the handle of the suitcase, finally realized he was in a whorehouse.

For Honour Mercy Bane, the last two weeks had been busy (though happily, not fruitful) ones. There'd been so much to learn, much more than she'd expected. It was, in many ways, more difficult to be a bad woman than to be a good woman. No good woman ever had to douche herself twenty times a day. No good woman had to keep smiling when her insides felt as though they'd been scraped with sandpaper; and here comes another one. No good woman had to try to be glamorous and desirable while doing the most unglamorous things in the world. Such as accepting money, and even sometimes (how silly could men get?) having to make change. Such as checking a man for external evidence of disease. Such as squatting over an enamel basin.

No good woman had to learn as much about the act of love, and its variations, as a bad woman did. And no good woman was exposed to quite so many variations all in one day.

Not that Honour Mercy Bane was unhappy in her chosen profession. Far from it. There were any number of things she enjoyed about it. First and foremost, of course, she enjoyed men. By the end of an eight-hour stint on her back, her enjoyment was usually on the wane, but she always snapped right back with it the next day, just as fresh and eager as ever.

And she liked the other girls, her coworkers. The other three girls on the night-shift with her were the ones she knew best, of course: Dee and Terri and Joan. Dee was a little difficult to understand, sometimes, with that big vocabulary of hers, but she was really friendly, and gave Honour Mercy a lot of good advice. Dee was a real pro, a girl who'd been working here for almost five years and knew just about everything there was to know about the business. Madge didn't know it, but Dee was saving up to start a house of her own. She talked with Madge a lot, finding out what it took to become a madam, who had to be paid off, the ins and outs of the trade. And Dee had promised that Honour Mercy could come with her when she set up her own place.

Joan was kind of strange, in a way. She never talked much, never seemed to care to go to the movies in the afternoon with the other girls or do anything, never seemed to care about anything but her eight hours a day at the Third Street Grill. She was friendly, but reserved, saving her smiles for her customers.

Terri was Honour Mercy's best friend of the bunch. Terri and she enjoyed the same things, loved to go to the matinees at the movie down the block from the hotel, loved to go window-shopping. They could talk together for hours without getting bored. Terri had come from the same kind of town and family as Honour Mercy, and for pretty much the same reason, and that made a bond of understanding between them.

As for Madge, Honour Mercy didn't see much difference between Madge and her parents back in Coldwater. They both had strict sets of rules and regulations, ironbound values, and absolutely insisted on complete obedience. Madge's set of rules and values was, of course, quite different from Honour Mercy's parents', and a lot easier to conform to, but the similarity was still there.

This was now her second Monday night, and her last night shift for two weeks. Starting tomorrow, she'd be on the noon-to-eight shift, which meant a little less money, but that was all right, because her period of forced inaction would come during that time. It would be better than being inactive while on the night shift, which was what kept happening to Terri.

In the last two weeks, she had come to learn that every man is different, and every man is the same. Every man is different in the preliminaries, and every man is the same in thinking that he is different in the act itself. At least twice a night, someone would come in with a brand-new variation he'd just thought up, and these variations were never brand new at all. Of course, Honour Mercy wouldn't tell the poor guy he wasn't as original as he thought he was. After all, it was extra money for extra service, and special tricks rated as extra service.

She had been worried that the other girls would get all the business, because they knew more, but it turned out that she got all the business she could handle. There was something naturally fresh and unspoiled and virginal about her, and a lot of men were attracted to that, liked to have the impression that they were the very first, though of course they had to know better, since she was working here and all. But still, they liked the impression, and she was making darn good money at it.

Of all the men who had come to see her in the last two weeks, this pop-eyed boy with the suitcase was by far the most different and most same one of them all. The fear and indecision and doubt that were, she knew, hidden deep in every man that paid his way here, was right out in the open on this boy's face. Sameness and difference. It was strange that a thing could be the same and different all at once.

She spoke to him, and he simply looked more pop-eyed than ever. Dee had told her, when a man got stage-fright in the parlor, bring him immediately upstairs. Seeing the bed will snap him out of it, one way or the other. Otherwise, you could waste half an hour with a man who might change his mind at the last minute and run off without paying a cent or doing a thing.

So Honour Mercy took the pop-eyed boy by the elbow, and gently led him upstairs. He followed obediently enough, but he didn't look any less terrified, no matter how much she smiled at him, or how gently she talked to him.

She led him to her room, empty except for the sheet-covered

bed and the stand and the chair and the enamel basin and the sink. And, upon seeing the bed, he froze solid.

"Come on, now, honey," she said soothingly. "It isn't as bad as all that. Why, some men even think it's fun. Specially when I do it with them. You come on, now."

He stayed frozen.

This was the first time a man had done this, but Honour Mercy was ready for it. Dee had warned her it might happen, and told her the antidote was nudity. She should take off her clothes, in front of him, as provocatively as possible.

She did. She crooned to him, telling him how much fun it would be, and she slipped out of her dress, wriggling her hips to make the dress slide down away from her body. Beneath the dress she wore only bra and panties. A slip was a waste of time, and a girdle would be a horror to remove.

She kicked off her shoes and walked over in front of the boy. "Unsnap me, will you?" she asked him, and turned her back.

She was afraid he'd stay frozen. If he didn't unsnap her, she didn't know exactly what she could do next. She waited, her back to him, holding her breath, and all at once she felt his fingers fumbling at the bra strap.

"That's a good boy, honey," she said. She turned to face him again, still smiling, and said, "Slip the old bra off me, will you, honey?"

His face was still frozen, but his arms seemed capable of movement. He reached up, gingerly, just barely touching her skin, and slid the bra straps down her arms, releasing the fullness of her breasts.

She cupped her hands under her breasts. "Do you like me?" she asked him. "Am I all right?"

He spoke for the first time, with something more like a frog-croak than a voice. "You're beautiful," he croaked, and his face turned red.

"Thank you," she murmured, and leaned forward to kiss his cheek, rubbing her body against him as she did. He stiffened again, and she swirled away, afraid of rushing him. She slid out of her panties, and walked, hip-rolling, toward him, her arms out to him. "Come on now," she crooned. "Come on now, honey, come on now."

His head was shaking back and forth. "I didn't know—" he started. "I thought—I didn't know—"

"Come on now, honey," she whispered, her outstretched arms almost reaching him.

"I can't!" he cried suddenly, and collapsed at her feet, sitting on the floor and covering his face with his hands.

She stared at him, amazed, and suddenly realized he was crying. A man, and he was crying. It was the strangest thing that ever happened.

She knelt on the floor beside him and put a protective arm around his shoulders. "That's all right, honey," she whispered. "That's all right."

"I can't," he said again, his voice muffled by his hands. "I can't, I can't, I can't. I've never done it, I've never, never done it. I don't know how, I can't—"

It seemed as though he'd go on that way forever. Honour Mercy interrupted him, saying, "If you never did, honey, how do you know you can't? There's a first time for everybody, you know. There was a first time for me."

Something—her voice, her words, her arm around his shoulder, she wasn't sure what had done it—something managed to calm him, and he looked at her with the most pathetic and wistful expression she had ever seen. Like a lost puppy, he was.

"I can show you how," she whispered. "It'll be all right, you'll see."

"I don't think I can," he said hopelessly.

"We'll try," she told him. "Here, I'll help you with your clothes."

Normally, she discouraged a man from undressing completely. It meant more time spent afterward, waiting for him to dress. But this, she knew, was a special case. This was the pop-eyed boy's first time, and she felt that it was her job to make it as good for him as she possibly could. She didn't stop to think that she was feeling this way solely because the boy was the first person she'd met in the last two weeks who was even less experienced than she.

She helped him undress, even to his socks, and they both looked at his body. "You see," he said mournfully. "I can't."

"Yes, you can," she said. "Come on to bed, and we'll take care of that."

Obediently, he crawled onto the bed with her, and they lay side by side. She touched him, holding him with one soft hand, and smiled at him. "I'll make you ready," she promised him. "Don't you worry."

"I want to," he said. "I really do, you're beautiful and I wish I could. But I just don't think I can."

"Yes, you can. Now, when you go downstairs, if Madge—that's

the heavy woman out front—if she asks you what you had, you tell her it was just a straight trick. That's ten dollars. You've got ten dollars, haven't you?"

He nodded vigorously.

"All right. You tell her it was just a straight trick." She smiled again, and squeezed him. "But it's going to be a lot more than that," she told him. Dee had told her how to get a man ready, all the different ways, and she did them all. At first, he lay awkwardly on his back, his brow furrowed with doubt and alarm, but gradually he relaxed to the soothing strokes of her voice and hands and lips. And all at once he was ready, and finished. It had happened like that, so fast, and he looked mournful all over again. But she whispered to him, fondled him, assured him it would be all right, and soon he was ready again, and this time it lasted. She didn't have to fake passion this time. Then he was finished again, completely finished this time, and they went through the mechanical aftermaths without losing any of the glow. He paid her the ten dollars, and she took him back downstairs, where she squeezed his hand and said, "You come back again, now, d'you hear?"

"I will," he said. "I sure will."

## Chapter 3

When she awoke she was not alone and for this she was very grateful. The monotonous walls of the hotel room were painted a dull gray that was no color at all and the made her feel trapped sometimes. A few pictures here and there might liven up the walls, and several times she had told herself to tear a picture or two from a magazine and get some scotch tape at Mr. Harris's drugstore on the corner, but she never remembered and the walls remained as depressing as ever. When she woke up they seemed to hem her in, and when she went to sleep they appeared to be watching her.

But now, now that she was no longer alone upon awakening, the walls were not nearly so hard to bear. Now that there was another warm body beside her own warm body, another human being sharing her bed, now everything was much more pleasant and it was a genuine joy to open her eyes and face the day.

She yawned a luxurious yawn with all her muscles participating. She stretched and yawned again. She closed her eyes and snuggled her face against the pillow that was warm with the cozy warmth of her own body heat.

When she opened her eyes again Richie was still in bed and still had not moved. She put her head on his chest and listened to his heart beating, listened to the rhythm of his breathing and smiled a slow and secret smile to herself. She put out a hand and touched his chest right over his heart, touched him once and just for a moment, and then removed her hand. He didn't move, didn't wake up, but he made a small sound through closed lips and he seemed to be smiling in his sleep.

*He's just a little boy,* she thought contentedly, and she put her head back on her warm pillow and closed her eyes again and thought about him, her little boy. She was glad that he was the way he was, that he was like a little boy and all afraid of everything and never quite sure what to do. He needed to be taken care of, needed her to hold him and cuddle him and watch him sleep, and for this she was thankful.

She remembered that time, the first time with him, and she remembered how he had been waiting for her when she left the house that night after work was finished. It was 4:30 in the morning by the time she got out of the house and the sun was getting ready to think about rising. The sky was light. The first birds were already out after the first worms and the ground was moist with dew.

She left the house and headed toward Schwerner Boulevard. She had walked maybe thirty yards when she heard a voice, a voice calling "Honey!" It was a few seconds before she realized that the voice was calling her because Honey was only her name during working hours, and that only with customers. Madge and Dee and Joan called her Honour. Terri, who seemed to think her full name was humorous, called her Honour Mercy, sometimes Honour Mercy Bane. She would drawl it out southern-fashion until even Honour Mercy, who thought her name a perfectly sensible one, would find herself laughing.

But now a voice was calling "Honey!" and the Honey it

referred to was quite obviously herself. She turned around and got scared for a minute because he was just a foot or two away from her, his eyes very intense, his mouth half-open and scared.

"Oh," she said. "It's you."

He seemed frightened by something, but after she took his arm he wasn't frightened any more. He told her that he had just come to town, that he didn't know where to go and that he didn't have any place to stay. She nodded thoughtfully, liking him and feeling sorry for him, and the two of them began walking toward Schwerner Boulevard. She was taking him to her hotel, although she did not know it at the time, and would have been surprised if someone had suggested it to her.

On the way he talked, talked about himself, and from the tone of his voice she got the feeling that he was telling her things he had never told anybody before, telling them to her without knowing why. Her customers often talked to her, sometimes before but more often afterward, but now it was not as if it was a customer talking to her. When the customers spoke she would nod her head and say "Uh-huh" without really hearing a word they spoke, but now she listened to everything he said. It was more like talking with one of the girls in the house but it wasn't quite like that either.

He told her that he was supposed to be with the Air Force at Scott Air Force Base near St. Louis. He told her that he was AWOL, that he had left without permission and would be punished if they caught him. He did not explain why he had left the base, not that night, although he did tell her several days later, but she knew then that he had done something wrong and that was why he had left.

She was glad to hear his confession. When he told her, she felt a kinship with him—they both had done something wrong and had been forced to run away. Neither of them could go back where they had come from. She was very glad, and when he told her she understood the similarity between them and she hugged his arm tighter.

At the entrance to the Casterbridge Hotel they stood awkwardly for a moment and he shifted from one foot to the other. Then she told him that he could stay with her for the night—or morning, more accurately—because it was no hour to go looking for a hotel room and because the police might arrest him if they found him out on the streets at that hour. He accepted gratefully and they went into the hotel and up the stairs and down the corridor to her little room.

In the room they got undressed and ready for bed and it was very funny to her. They undressed and they were not unaware of each other or embarrassed by each other. They were two human beings undressing and getting ready for bed and it was an extremely natural thing.

She turned out the light and they got into the little bed. It was a small bed and they were very close together and each was very conscious of the presence of the other. At first she lay down with her back toward him, but then she rolled over and let him take her in his arms. He kissed her and he did it very awkwardly because he did not know anything about kissing. It was the one thing she had not shown him that night, and he did it badly as a result, but she didn't mind because she thought it was cute the way his nose pressed against hers and the way his hands on her back moved shakily and nervously.

Then she showed him how to kiss, how to make his mouth behave the way his mind wanted it to behave, and they lay very still holding each other and kissing each other, lips gentle and tongues explorative. His hands examined her body with a combination of wonder and admiration and he murmured "Honey, Honey, Honey!" into her chestnut hair.

She told him her name was really Honour Mercy, and after that he never called her Honey again but always called her Honour Mercy. He always used both names, but when he said it it never sounded funny the way it did when Terri said it.

They did not make love that night. That is, they did not take possession of one another. In a larger sense they made love much more certainly than two strangers who copulated. They held each other close all night through, and while both of them were far too tired for intercourse, their simple presence together was a full and satisfying act of love.

She had been the first woman for him and she was glad, glad that it had been she who taught him how to love. Other women are generally grateful for a man's experience rather than for the lack of it, but for her it was the other way around. She had already decided that experience wasn't particularly important, that one man was quite like another in bed, that the ones who had done the most and bragged the loudest were usually the most disappointing. Men seemed to think that their prowess hinged upon the length of time they could sustain intercourse, and the variations with which they were acquainted.

Other things were more important: the joy Richie took in her body and in his own, the happiness she was able to bring him, the shy smile on his young face and the mistiness in the corners of his eyes, the way he held her hand. Another man, while he knew seventeen variations on the old theme and could sustain the act almost indefinitely, never could make her feel the way Richie did.

And so she was glad she had been the first for him. In another way he was the first for her.

He was the first man she ever slept with.

When she went to work the next day at noon, he took her work for granted just as she took it for granted that he would be there when she returned. The two of them moved into another room on the same floor of the Casterbridge Hotel, a larger room with a double bed, and that night he unpacked his suitcase and hung his Air Force uniform on a hanger in the closet.

They never talked about her work. It was her job, a well-paying job and a job she enjoyed, and in his mind as well as hers it was completely divorced from their life together. He accepted it so completely that it was unnecessary to talk about it. In turn she accepted the fact that he had to stay in the hotel room as much of the time as possible, that he couldn't get a job or spend much time out of doors because the Air Police might be looking for him. She put in eight hours a day at the house, and during those eight hours he read the paperback novels and detective magazines that she bought for him at the drugstore. She thought now that she would have to remember to get him some more magazines on her way home from work, and reminded herself that she ought to pick up a roll of scotch tape at the same time and put some pictures up to make the room nicer.

She ran her hand over his chest, stroked his stomach, felt him wake up ready for her and wanting her. His eyes never opened but he didn't have to have his eyes open to reach for her, to hold her and whisper her name and move with her and against her, and love her.

It was over quickly but not too quickly. It was the way it should be, with him still drugged with sleep and her still not fully awake, and when it was over he kept his eyes closed and his heart was beating rapidly and his chest heaving. Then, his eyes still shut, he rolled free of her and lay on his own pillow, face downward this time. Seconds later he was asleep once more.

She looked at him for several minutes, her eyes filled with the love of him and the need for him, her body thoroughly satisfied and her mind happy. She was smiling now without realizing it and the smile remained on her face as she slipped out from under the thin blanket and tiptoed to the bathroom. She showered and stepped out of the shower and dried herself on one of the hotel's towels, which were too small and not absorbent enough, and reminded herself that she really ought to buy some good towels on sale for 49¢ and it would be worth it to have a towel that really got you dry.

She dressed quickly but carefully. She put on a pair of panties and a bra and a frilly green dress that went well with her hair. The dress was cut low and the bra showed so she slipped out of the dress, shed the bra and put the dress on again. She checked herself in the mirror—her breasts showed a little but not too much and it made her sexy without looking cheap. Madge was very firm on that point. She said that when a man paid ten dollars or more he deserved a girl who looked classy.

When she was fully dressed she looked at the little alarm clock on the night-table. It was 11:45 and she had to hurry. It was time for her to go to work.

•     •     •

If Richie Parsons had one regret it was that he couldn't sleep fifteen hours a day.

He slept with Honour Mercy. When she came back to the hotel room, at 4:30 in the morning if she was working nights, and at 8:30 in the evening if she was working the early shift, they were together talking and eating and just plain being together until it was time for her to sleep. If she worked the early shift, they went to sleep around three in the morning; when she worked nights, they went to sleep between five and six. When he was asleep it was good because she was in the bed with him, and when they were together it was good simply because it was always good when they were together. But for eight hours every day—and closer to nine hours, what with her leaving a little early and staying at the house a little late—he was alone by himself in the hotel room, alone with some paperback novels and detective magazines.

Richie never cared too much for reading. The only reason he read the paperback novels and the detective magazines was that there was very little else to do when you were cooped up in a hotel room for eight hours. So he read the novels and magazines and played solitaire. Honour Mercy had brought him a deck of playing cards once, a fancy deck that one of her customers had given her for a joke with a different pornographic illustration on the back of each of the fifty-two cards, and for a time he played solitaire constantly when she was gone. He even made a running game out of it, keeping careful score of how many games he played and how many he won on a scrap of paper, but after a while it became far more monotonous than the paperback novels or the detective magazines. He only knew one game of solitaire and it wasn't a particularly complex one, so after a week or so he stopped playing.

The pictures on the backs of the cards, which had been a source of interest and amusement for a time, were now too familiar to arouse his attention. The playing cards alone would have driven him insane with desire before he met Honour Mercy, but now that he had a completely satisfactory sexual relationship the pictures were not exciting in the least. He didn't need pictures any more.

It was twelve-thirty before he got up that afternoon and he wished he could have remained unconscious until half-past-eight when Honour Mercy would come back to the room. But finally he couldn't sleep any longer and he got out of bed, rubbed the sleep from his eyes and went to the bathroom to shave and shower and brush his teeth. He put on a worn flannel shirt and a pair of dungarees and went downstairs for breakfast.

Gil Gluck, who owned the Casterbridge Hotel, also owned a luncheonette around the corner where Richie Parsons had his breakfast each day. If there was one characteristic that distinguished the lunch counter from any other in Newport, it was the fact that Gil Gluck conducted no other *sub rosa* business there. There were no rooms behind the lunch counter where harlots entertained men, no rooms where men wore green eyeshades and dealt cards around tables, no rooms where bootleg moonshine was sold or white powder peddled. The Canarsie Grille, endowed with the name of Gil Gluck's beloved hometown and spelled "grille" because the sign-painter Gil Gluck had hired was an incurable romantic, dealt solely in such eminently respectable commodities as eggs, wheat cakes, coffee, hamburgers, home fries, Coca Cola and the like.

The fact that the Canarsie Grille was plain and simple, a luncheonette, the fact that there was nothing at all illegal in Gil Gluck's operations either in the luncheonette or in the hotel, was a source of tremendous consternation to the police force of Newport. Time and time again they had pulled surprise raids on first the hotel and then the Canarsie Grille; time and again they had found nothing more incriminating than a roach in a closet or a dirty spoon in a drawer.

Since the roach in the closet was a bewildered cockroach and not the butt of a marijuana cigarette, since no heroin had been cooked in the spoon, there was nothing the police could do. Gil Gluck paid the police nothing, and this bothered them. While metropolitan police, a far more sophisticated breed, would have found a way to squeeze money out of Gil Gluck, come hell or high water, no matter how honest he was, the Newport police cursed softly under their collective breath and let him alone. They also drank coffee there, since Gil was the only man in town who made a really good cup of coffee.

Richie Parsons drank coffee at the Canarsie Grille. He drank it with two spoonful's of sugar and enough cream to kill the taste of Gil's good coffee. This bothered Gil, who was justly proud of his coffee. But the fact that Richie always ordered wheat cakes, and licked his lips appreciatively after the first bite, endeared him to Gil.

The fact that Gil was a regular customer of Honour Mercy's might not have endeared the little bald man to Richie, but it was a fact that Gil Gluck sagely refrained from mentioning to the boy.

Richie finished the last of the wheat cakes and poured the rest of the coffee down his throat. He put the cup back in the saucer, then raised it a few inches to indicate that he wanted another cup. Gil took his cup, rinsed it out in the sink and filled it with coffee. He brought it to Richie, who in turn polluted it with cream and sugar and sipped at it. It tasted good and he took a cigarette from his pocket and lit it to go with the coffee.

When the cop came in and sat down next to him, Richie was suddenly scared stiff.

The cop was a big man. Richie didn't dare to look at him but he could see the cop's face out of the corner of his eye. It was composed primarily of chin. Richie could also see the cop's holster out of the corner of his eye, the black leather holster with the .38 police positive in it. The gun, to Richie at least, was composed primarily of bullets, bullets which could splatter Richie to hell.

Richie sat there on his stool, the cup of coffee frozen halfway between saucer and mouth, the cigarette clutched so tightly between his fingers that it was a wonder it didn't snap in two. Richie sat there terrified, waiting for something to happen.

Gil Gluck came over and stood in front of the cop.

Gil Gluck said: "What'll you have?"

"Coffee," said the cop.

Gil brought the coffee. The cop, who liked coffee and who appreciated good coffee, drank the coffee black and without sugar. He smacked his lips over the coffee and Gil Gluck glowed.

"Nice day," said the cop.

"If it don't rain," said Gil, who had absorbed the subtleties of Kentucky conversation.

"You sure ought to open up a game in that back room of yours," said the cop, for perhaps the eightieth time. "Be a natural."

Gil let it ride. "How's business?"

The cop shrugged. "Usual."

"Anybody get killed?"

The cop laughed, thinking that Gil sure had a sense of humor. "Usual," he repeated. "Hold-up over on Grant Street but the jackass who stuck the place up ran out of the store and smack into a cop. He didn't get ten yards out of the store before he had handcuffs on him."

"What kind of store?"

"Liquor store," said the cop. "Grobers package store. Up near Tenth Street on the downtown side. Know the place?"

"Sure."

"Well, that's all we had. Oh, there was a jailbreak down in Louisville and we got a few wanted posters on it. And an out-of-state air force base sent down a picture of a deserter they figure headed this way, but that's just the ordinary stuff. Nothing much is happening in Newport."

Richie Parsons went numb.

What Richie Parsons did not know, although any jackass ought to have been able to figure it out, was that the out-of-state air force base the cop was referring to was Wright-Patterson Air Force Base in Dayton, Ohio. Scott Air Force Base would hardly bother sending wanted notices as far as Newport. But to Richie Parsons, who had been born scared, any mention of a deserter was sufficient cause to crawl under the nearest rotting log and await Armageddon.

The deserter that the Wright-Patterson people were looking

for was not at all similar to Richie Parsons. His name was Warren Michael Stults, he was twenty-three years old, six foot three and built like a Sherman tank. He was being searched for not only because he had gone over the hill but also because, as a prelude to desertion, he had kicked the hell out of his commanding officer. The commanding officer, bemoaning the loss of three front teeth and a goodly amount of self-respect, wanted to get hold of Warren Michael Stults as soon as possible.

But Richie Parsons did not know this angle.

And Richie Parsons was scared green.

He put money on the Formica top of the counter for his breakfast and edged out of the Canarsie Grille. The familiar skulk was back in his step and the familiar look of barely restrained terror was back on his face. The door stuck when he tried to open it and he almost fainted dead away on the spot. But he got through the door without attracting any attention and scurried around to the hotel.

The cop had noticed him, however. "What's with him?" the cop wondered aloud after Richie was gone.

"Him?"

"The little guy," the cop said. "The one who just scurried out of here with his tail between his legs."

"Oh," said Gil.

"He new around here?"

"He lives up at the hotel," Gil said. "Been here about a month."

"What's he do for a living?"

"Lives with one of the whores," Gil said.

"He pimp for her?"

"Must," said Gil, who couldn't imagine a man living with a whore and not pimping for her.

"Good for him," the cop said. "At least he's making an honest living. It's guys like you who give this town a lousy reputation."

Gil smiled—an infinitely patient smile—and filled the cop's cup with more black coffee.

The hell of it was that he had read all of the books and magazines in the room.

That's what made it so impossible. Seven hours in an empty hotel room is a bore, whatever way you look at it, but it would have been a lot easier to bear if he had a book or magazine to read. As it was, the room was full of books and magazines but he had read every last one of them.

He couldn't go out of the room. That much was obvious. He couldn't go out, not even to the drugstore to buy himself something to read, not even down to the Canarsie Grille later on for another cup of coffee. There were candy bars at the hotel desk, but he was too petrified to chance going downstairs again, so he did nothing but sit in his room in the hotel, going quietly out of his mind.

Newport was not safe anymore. In his mind he saw every policeman in the town studying his picture with interest and devoting every minute of his time to a careful search for *Richie Parsons, Deserter.* Just as it never entered his mind that the deserter could be anyone but him, it never occurred to him that the Newport police couldn't care less about an out-of-state deserter, that they

got a notice like that every day of every week, and that the cop
had mentioned it solely to show what a bore the day was.

Richie knew only that he was a hunted man.

The fact that he remained for seven-and-a-half terror-stricken
hours in room 26 of the Hotel Casterbridge is striking testimony
to the hold Honour Mercy Bane had upon him. If it were not for
her, he would have been on the first bus or train out of Newport.
No, that's not right—he wouldn't have chanced recognition at
the bus or train station, fearing that the police would be watching
such areas of escape. He would have hiked clear to the city limits
of Cincinnati and then hitched a ride.

But not now. Now he had to wait for Honour Mercy because
he could not possibly leave without her.

He got the deck of cards, shuffled them and began to deal out
a hand of solitaire. He had to cheat once or twice, but he won
three games straight before it became so boring that he couldn't
stand it. Then he ran through the deck and observed the posi-
tions of the men and women on the back of each card, trying to
take some vicarious interest in their obvious celluloid joy, but
they left him cold.

He put the cards down and sat in a chair facing the door. At
any moment he expected a knock, but after a half-hour his fear
changed its manifestation from nervousness to a strange calm.
Instead of fidgeting, he sat stiff as a board and waited for time
to pass, waited for it to be eight-thirty and for Honour Mercy
to come home so that they could get the hell out of the town of
Newport.

He barely moved at all. Periodically he lit a cigarette,

periodically he ducked ashes on the rug, periodically he dropped the cigarette to the floor and stepped on it.

And periodically he wiped the cold sweat from his forehead.


Honour Mercy Bane was tired.

She was tired because, for an early shift, there had been one hell of a lot of action. It had been a back-breaking day which had culminated in a thirty-five-dollar trick at five minutes to eight, and now that she was out of the place she felt she would be happy never to see the inside of a house again.

She was hungry but she didn't stop for a bite to eat, preferring to wait and have supper with Richie. She didn't forget to buy magazines and books for him, but she was in such a hurry to get home that she remembered the books and magazines and passed the drugstore anyhow, figuring that she could get them later.

She had to get back to the hotel room in a hurry. She didn't know why, but she had a strange feeling that the faster she saw Richie, the better.

When she opened the door of the room he straightened up in the chair and his eyes were wide. Before she could say anything, he stood up and motioned for her to shut the door. She did so, puzzled.

"We have to leave," he said.

She looked at him.

"They're looking for me," he said, "and we've got to get out of town."

She nodded. She thought that Madge would be disappointed

when she didn't show up at the house the following day, that Terri would miss her and that some of her steadies would grumble when they discovered she was literally nowhere to be had. But the thought of remaining in Newport never entered her mind.

"Better start packing."

She got her ratty cardboard suitcase from the closet and spread it on the bed and began filling it with clothes. At the same time, he packed his own suitcase, and the first thing he put into it was his uniform.

She had, fortunately, quite a lot of money. There was good money to be made at a Newport whorehouse and she had been making it. Neither she nor Richie could be classed as a big spender and she had over four hundred dollars in her purse. That, she thought, ought to be enough to last them quite a time.

She packed up her dresses and they were much nicer than the clothing she had carried with her from Clearwater. She didn't have room for everything in the little suitcase and had to leave some of the dresses behind, but she managed to take along the ones she liked best.

They packed in a hurry. It didn't take them more than fifteen minutes all told before both suitcases were jammed and lay ready to go. Then she went to Richie and he took her in his arms and held her very close and kissed her several times, his arms holding her firmly and tenderly. When he held her like that, and kissed her like that, he didn't seem scared at all.

And when he did that, the memory of that last thirty-five-dollar trick was washed out of her system. She completely forgot about it.

Then he let go of her. There would be time later to make love, plenty of time when they were out of Newport and out of Kentucky and away someplace safe. She picked up her suitcase and he picked up his suitcase and they walked out of the room and down the stairs and out of the hotel. If Richie skulked as he walked, his thin body hugging the sides of the buildings they passed, Honour Mercy Bane didn't notice it.

He would not hitchhike, not with her along, and they were walking to the bus station. She wondered what it would be like where they were going. She had not asked him where they were headed and did not have the slightest idea whether he was taking her north or south or east or west.

She was like Ruth in the Bible that Prudence and Abraham Bane read from every day of their lives. Wherever he took her she would go.

# CHAPTER 4

It was well after midnight, and the bus, mumbling to itself, rolled steadily northward, toward Cleveland, leaving Cincinnati far to the south behind it. Ohio is built something like a grandfather clock. At the top is Cleveland, the clock-face, and at the bottom is Cincinnati, the pendulum-weight, and in between there isn't very much of anything. In the middle of the night, there's even less.

Most of the people on the bus were asleep. Honour Mercy was asleep, her head, in a mute declaration of alliance, resting comfortably against Richie Parsons' shoulder. Only three people in the whole bus were awake. One of them, fortunately, was the driver, up front there. The second was a soft guitar-player, sitting way in back and singing quietly to himself: "You will eat, you will eat, by and by; In that glorious land in the sky, way up high; Work and pray, live on hay; You'll get pie in the sky when you die. That's a lie."

It was a soothingly quiet guitar, and a soothingly quiet voice, and it helped, with the vibration of the bus, in putting everybody asleep. But it didn't soothe Richie Parsons. He was wide awake, and the song sounded ominous to him. At that point, any song would have sounded ominous to him.

He was thinking of the fiasco he had made of buying the ticket. The thing was, he didn't *plan*. He just stumbled ahead, willy-nilly, hoping for the best, and every once in a while a chasm opened up in front of him.

A chasm had opened at the ticket window in Newport. The thing was, Richie just wasn't a world traveler. His entire traveling history had been similar to the traveling of a yo-yo. He traveled *from* home *to* someplace else, or *from* someplace else *to* home.

Besides which, he hadn't thought about a destination. He had thought only about leaving Newport, not at all about going somewhere else.

So when he stood in front of the ticket window at the bus depot, he said it automatically, without stopping to think about it at all. "Two tickets to Albany," he said, and the chasm opened up as big as life and twice as deep.

He couldn't go to Albany! That was where he lived, for the love of Pete, he couldn't go there!

But he'd already said it, and he was now too petrified to say anything else, to change the already announced destination. To be a draft-age young man on the way to Albany was suspicious enough. To be a draft-age young man who changed his mind and decided not to go to Albany after all wasn't suspicious, it was an absolute admission of identity.

While teetering on the brink of the chasm, he heard the calm (not suspicious!) voice of the ticket agent say, "One way or round trip?"

With the impulsive cunning of a treed raccoon, he said, "Round trip." There, that would allay the ticket agent's suspicions.

Two round-trip tickets to Albany cost him a hundred dollars

and change. It was a pretty expensive way to allay suspicions, all things considered, depleting their finances by one-quarter.

He was too embarrassed and ashamed to tell Honour Mercy what he'd done. Happily, she didn't ask him where they were going, and the public address system, in announcing their bus, mentioned so many other cities (Cleveland, Pittsburg, Harrisburg, Philadelphia) that his blunder was lost in the crowd.

So here he was on the bus, well after midnight, surrounded by gently snoring (innocent, untroubled) passengers, being serenaded with songs about death, and hurtling toward doom and destruction and Albany.

What to do? He considered leaving the bus at one of the cities before Albany, and rejected it. The driver, who kept a head-count, would notice that two passengers were missing, and would delay the bus for them, for a few minutes, thereby calling attention to their absence. The Authorities would somehow get into the act, and Richie could visualize the scene in which the driver described the runaways to these Authorities, who wouldn't take long to realize that the absent male was none other than the deserter from Scott Air Force Base, Richie Parsons.

He couldn't stay on the bus all the way to Albany, and he couldn't leave it beforehand. The problem was too much for him. He stared gloomily at the night-shrouded empty flatness outside the window, and the guitarist in the back seat switched to a new song: "Hang down your head, Tom Dooley; Hang down your head and cry; Hang down your head, Tom Dooley; Poor boy, you're bound to die."

It was a long night.

They had breakfast in Cleveland, where Richie was too

nervous to operate the silverware, and Honour Mercy finally asked him what was wrong. It was obvious he hadn't slept all night.

So he admitted his mistake, shame-facedly, and outlined the horns of the dilemma. And Honour Mercy, the practical one, immediately gave him the solution. "We change buses in New York," she said. "We just won't change, that's all. People do it all the time. Get later buses and things."

Richie smiled with sudden relief. "Sure," he said. "Sure!" And when they got back on the bus, he fell immediately to sleep.

He woke up to discover that the bus was inside a building, with a lot of other buses, and the confining walls and roof made the sound of all those engines a tremendous racket.

He didn't know where he was, or where in the world he possibly could be, and the panic that always rode just beneath his surface popped out again, and he stared around in absolute terror.

Fortunately for Richie Parsons, Honour Mercy Bane was a girl loaded to the gunwales with maternal instinct. She now put a soothing hand on his arm, and told him, quietly, that they were in New York City and this was the bus depot. "I didn't know whether I should wake you up to see everything when we came into the city or not," she added. "But you looked so peaceful, sleeping there, I thought I should let you alone."

"You can just disappear in New York," Richie told her. "It's so big." He'd read that someplace, and firmly believed it.

People were getting off the bus. Richie blocked the aisle for a minute, getting the two suitcases down from the overhead rack, and then he and Honour Mercy followed the other passengers into the brightly-lit main waiting room of the Port Authority bus terminal. Honour Mercy, this last part of the trip, had been thinking again about finances. Four hundred dollars—now three hundred dollars—seemed like an awful lot when your chief expenses were magazines and paperback books and other items from the drugstore, and meals. But three hundred dollars seemed like an awfully small drop in an awfully big bucket when it was all you had to live on in New York City. Somebody had told her that living New York was more expensive than anyplace else in the world, and she believed that as firmly as Richie believed that it was possible to just disappear in New York.

They had an awful lot of money tied up in two tickets from Albany to Newport, two cities neither of them expected to be going to for some time. It seemed wasteful, and Honour Mercy, if she retained nothing else from Abraham and Prudence Bane, her begetters, retained a rock-like sense of thrift.

In the middle of the waiting room, she made her decision. "Give me the return tickets, Richie," she said. "I'll go see if I can turn them in."

Richie considered for a second. The Air Police weren't looking for a girl. "Okay," he said. He handed her the tickets, and she went off to find the right window.

That wasn't too easy. She'd never known so many bus companies were in existence, and every window was for another group of them. But she finally found the right one, and turned the tickets in, explaining that she wasn't going back to Newport after all. The man at the window had her fill out a slip of paper, to which she affixed a false name, and ungrumblingly gave her almost forty dollars.

She returned to Richie to find him quaking in his boots. Two young men in uniform, one an Air Policeman and the other an Army Military Policeman, were strolling slowly around the waiting room, like casual friends on a promenade.

Honour Mercy took Richie's trembling arm. "Act natural," she whispered, which only made him look more terrified than ever, and she led him past the Authorities and out the door to New York's Eighth Avenue.

It was five p.m. and the rush hour. They stood on the sidewalk on Eighth Avenue, between 40th and 41st Streets, and watched the mobs of people rushing by in both directions, bumping into one another and rushing on with neither apology nor annoyance. It was obvious a Martian in a flying saucer could disappear in a crowd like that. Certainly Richie Parsons, who was practically invisible to begin with, could disappear in that multidirectional stream with no trouble at all.

They turned left, because the choice was between left and right and one was just as good as another, and joined the herd. They crossed 42nd Street, and kept on going northward, purposeless at the moment, following the momentum of the crowd and waiting for something to happen.

The crowd thinned out above 42nd Street, and they could walk more easily, without a lot of shoulder-bumping and dodging around. Honour Mercy was keeping an eye out for a hotel, which was their first concern, and saw a huge block-square hotel between 44th and 45th Streets, with a uniformed doorman and a curb lined with late-model cars. That wasn't exactly the kind of hotel she had in mind. They kept on walking.

At 47th Street, they saw a hotel sign down to their left, toward Ninth Avenue. This was the kind of hotel she had in mind. It was made up of three tenement buildings, five stories high, combined into one building, with the same ancient coat of gray paint on the faces of all three. The entrances of the flanking buildings had been removed, replaced by windows indicating that additional rooms had been set up where the entranceways had been, leaving the front door of the middle building as the only remaining entrance to the hotel. A square sign, white on black, stuck out over the street, saying simply, "HOTEL," not even gracing the place with a name.

"Down this way," she told Richie, and gently steered him around the corner. He saw the hotel sign then, and homed on it gratefully, anxious to have once more the sanctuary of four peeling walls around him.

The hotel didn't have a lobby, all it had was a first-floor hall, with stairs leading upward, a few dim light bulbs ineffectually battling the interior darkness, and frayed maroon carpeting on the floor and staircase. Just to the right of the entrance was a door to what had probably been the front apartment, when this building had been a separate entity and not yet a hotel. There was only the bottom half of a door there now, with a board about ten inches wide across the top of this half-door, and a grizzled, grimy old man leaning on the board, his elbows between the registry book and the telephone.

Honour Mercy, knowing Richie would be unable to effectively go through the process of renting a room, did the talking. The old man didn't bother to ask if they were married, and didn't bother to look at the false names Honour Mercy wrote in his registry book. He asked for fourteen dollars for a week's rent, gave

Honour Mercy a receipt and two keys, told her room 26 was on the third floor, off to the right, and that was that.

They climbed the creaking stairs to the third floor, and turned right. The hall, narrow and dim-lit, passed through an amateurishly breached wall into the next building over, and at the end of it, left side, was room 26. Honour Mercy unlocked the door, and they walked into their new home.

It was a step down from the Casterbridge Hotel, back in Newport. The walls were almost precisely the same color, which didn't help, and the one window looked out on the back of a building on the next block. The dresser was ancient and scarred and sagging, the closet had no door on it, and the ceiling was peeling, as though it had a gray-white sunburn. There was a double-bed in the room, which would perhaps be a bit more comfortable than the single bed they'd shared at the Casterbridge, but that was the only good thing in sight.

They unpacked, trying to get some of their own individuality into the room just as rapidly as possible, and a couple of brown bugs dashed away down the wall when Honour Mercy opened the dresser drawers. Before she could get at them with a shoe heel, they'd disappeared under the molding. The Casterbridge Hotel hadn't had bugs, and no one had prepared her for the fact that New York City was infested from top to bottom with cockroaches, nasty little brown bugs with lots of legs and hard shell-like backs, who took one generation to build up immunity to virtually any poison used against them, which made their extermination more wishful thinking than practical reality.

The sight of the bugs made Honour Mercy want to get out of there for a while. They could come back when it was dark. She had a childish faith in the power of electric light to keep bugs from venturing out of their crannies in the walls.

Richie was torn between the desire to just sit down in the middle of the room and breathe easily for a day or two and a hunger that had been building since Cleveland. The hunger, aided by Honour Mercy's prodding, won out, and they left the hotel to find a place to eat.

They had dinner at a luncheonette on the corner of 46th and Eighth, and then went back to the hotel. It was dark now, and Honour Mercy hopefully turned on the bare bulb in a ceiling fixture which was their only light source. The bulb, in an economy move on the part of the management, was forty watts, and gave a smoky light not quite good enough to read by.

They sat around on the bed, digesting and talking lazily together about their successful flight from Newport. After a while, Honour Mercy spread their money out on the blanket and counted it, finding they still had a little over three hundred dollars. At fourteen dollars a week for the hotel room, and the cost of food, and movies or whatever to fill their time, it wouldn't take long for that three hundred dollars to be all gone.

There was only one sensible thing to do. She should go back to work right now, while they still had some money ahead, rather than wait until they were broke. The idea of having money ahead, in case of emergencies of one sort or another, appealed to Honour Mercy both as a child of thrifty parents and a girl in a risky line of work.

A little after ten, she gave Richie two dollars and told him to go to a movie for a while. They'd seen a whole line of movie marquees on 42nd Street, on their way to the hotel, and Honour

Mercy was sure she'd heard or read somewhere that 42nd Street movies in New York City were open all night long. And if she were going to go back to work, she would need a room with a bed in it. She was pretty sure this was the kind of hotel where she could carry on her trade unquestioned.

Richie was reluctant to leave the room. In the first place, the outside world was heavily patrolled by policemen of all kinds; city police, state troopers, Air Police, FBI agents, Shore Patrol, Military Police, and the Lord knew what else. In the second place, the idea of Honour Mercy bringing work home served only to force the nature of her work—which was supporting him—right out into the open, where he had to look at it. Back in Newport, Honour Mercy was "away at work" eight or nine hours a day, and he could more or less ignore the facts of the work. Here, *he* was going to have to be away, while Honour Mercy worked here, right on this bed. It made a difference.

"Don't be silly," she told him. "You certainly can't get a job, at least not yet, not until you've been gone long enough for everybody to have forgotten all about you. And there's only one way I can earn enough money for both of us to live on. And besides that, I really don't mind it. It isn't the same as with us, you know that, it's just what I do, that's all."

It took her half an hour to soothe his newly-risen male pride and hurt self-respect, but finally he admitted that she was the practical one and he would follow her lead, and he went off to the movies, skulking along next to walls.

Honour Mercy's next problem was one of location. Back in Newport, there'd been no problem about where to go to find work. One just went downtown, that was all. But New York was a different matter. To the new arrival, New York seemed to be one giant downtown, extending for miles in all directions. Now where, in all of that, was the section where Honour Mercy's trade was plied?

Honour Mercy didn't know it yet, but she was lucky as to location. Eighth Avenue, in the Forties, is one of New York's centers of ambulatory whoredom. Just a block away, on 46th Street, there were a couple of bars, interspersed with legitimate taverns and restaurants, which specialized in receiving telephone calls for predominantly feminine clientele. The building in back which she could look at from her window was jam-packed with whores, most of whom were at the moment making exactly the same preparations Honour Mercy was making in the communal bathroom down the hall from room 26.

So Honour Mercy wasn't going to have to walk very far.

She left the hotel a little after eleven, and started retracing her steps toward 42nd Street, which had looked more downtowny than anything else she'd seen so far in New York, and which therefore seemed like the best place from which to start her search for Whore Row.

She found it sooner than that. The corner of 46th and Eighth was a poor man's Hollywood and Vine. Girls were going by in all directions, singly and in pairs, and their faces and clothing told Honour Mercy immediately that she had found the right place.

That was nice, she thought. It was handy to the hotel.

She walked around a bit, looking at things. It was still pretty early, and the middle of the week besides, and there wasn't much doing just yet. So she just looked at everything, wanting to familiarize herself with the locals and local methods just as soon as possible.

Then a woman holding up a wall on 46th Street called to her, and motioned her to come over for a talk. Honour Mercy, wondering what this was all about, complied.

The woman, without preamble, said, "You just get into town?" She looked to be in her late twenties, with frizzy black hair that stuck out in wire-like waves from her head, and much too much makeup on her eyes.

Honour Mercy nodded.

"Who you working with?" asked the woman.

"Nobody," admitted Honour Mercy. "I just got here." Remembering that Newport hadn't liked the girl who hustled on her own, without the blessing of one of the established houses, and assuming that New York would probably be much the same, she added, "I've been looking around for somebody to show me what to do. I just got here today, and I don't know New York at all."

"You found me," said the woman. She left the wall, which didn't topple over, and took Honour Mercy's arm. "And it's a good thing you did," she said, leading Honour Mercy down 46th Street, away from Eighth Avenue. "The cops would've picked you up in no time. They got to make some arrests, you know, so they're always on the lookout for strays."

"I didn't know," said Honour Mercy humbly, showing her willingness to learn and to adapt.

The woman took her into the building Honour Mercy could see from her hotel window, and up the stairs to a room on the second floor. The room was severely functional. It contained a bed and a kitchen chair, and that was all.

"My name's Marie," said the woman, sitting down on the bed.

"Honey," said Honour Mercy.

"Glad to know you. I'll introduce you to a couple people after a while. They'll explain the set-up to you. Good-looking girl like you, they'll probably put you on the phone."

"Thanks," said Honour Mercy.

"Of course," said Marie, grinning a little, "I can't just recommend you out of hand. You know what I mean: I got to be sure you're okay. I tell you what, you take off your clothes. Let's see what you got to offer."

Honour Mercy's reaction to that was complex, and it would be impossible to give the succession of her thoughts as rapidly as she thought them. Within a second, her thoughts passed from recognition through memory to decision, and with hardly a pause at all, she acted on the decision.

Here were the thoughts: Recognition. Marie was a lesbian. Honour Mercy knew it as surely as she knew anything in the world. The unnecessarily tight grip on her arm as they came up the stairs together. The unnecessary demand that she take off her clothes. Marie was a lesbian, and the price of her introducing Honour Mercy to the people who could give the unofficial blessing to her working in her occupation here in New York was that Honour Mercy be lesbian with her for a few minutes.

Memory. The girls in Newport had talked about lesbians more than once. It was a problem girls in their trade had to think about. In the first place, a surprisingly large percentage of prostitutes became lesbian, at one point or another. Since they got from men only sex without love, they tried to get sex *with* love from other women. In the second place, Madge had been one hundred percent opposed to hiring lesbians, on the grounds that dykes couldn't give a man as good a time as a normal woman could.

Decision. Sex was Honour Mercy's stock in trade. It was the way she made her living. With the help of Richie Parsons, she had successfully severed sex from love, without severing love from sex. She gave her body to men so she could have money to support herself and Richie. It wasn't really such a large step further to give her body to a woman so she could have the right to work.

She took off her clothes. The woman kept grinning at her, and said, "You know what I have in mind, Honey?"

"Sure," said Honour Mercy. She said it as casually as possible, not wanting this Marie to get the idea that Honour Mercy thought the whole thing repugnant. That might spoil everything.

Marie's grin now turned into an honest smile, and she joined Honour Mercy in the disrobing. They lay down together on the bed, and out of the corner of her eye Honour Mercy saw one of the brown bugs run out of a crack in the wall and diagonally down to the molding, where he disappeared again. She closed her eyes, struggling to keep her face expressionless, and Marie leaned over to kiss her on the mouth.

Having sex with a woman, Honour Mercy decided later, wasn't having sex at all. It was just having a lot of preliminaries, all jumbled up together, and then stopping just when things were getting interesting.

Marie got a lot more excited than Honour Mercy did. She squirmed and writhed around, and somehow she managed to build herself up to a climax. Honour Mercy, thinking it was expected of her, made believe she had one, too; and then Marie, as satisfied as any of Honour Mercy's satisfied customers, crawled off and started to dress.

Honour Mercy wanted to wash, very badly, but she thought it would give the wrong impression to mention it, so she didn't say anything. She just dressed again, and waited for Marie to tell her what was next.

"That was fun, huh, Honey?" said Marie, and she patted Honour Mercy on the behind. Her hand lingered, and Honour Mercy unobtrusively moved out of reach.

"We'll have to see each other some more," said Marie. She came closer and took Honour Mercy's arm, again with the unnecessary tightness, and said, "Now let's go see a man about a whore."

CHAPTER 5

When Joshua Crawford was a little boy his name was not Joshua Crawford. The Joshua part had been with him all his life, but the Crawford part had become his when he made out his diploma a few days before graduation from PS 105 on Hester Street.

The teacher, a sad-faced man with fallen arches and red-rimmed eyes, went through the traditional pre-diploma rites of New York's lower East side. "You may now, for probably the last time, change your names without the formality of a court order," he intoned. "This is the last chance for all Isaacs to become Irving, for all Moshes to become Morris, for all Samuels to become Sidney." And all the Isaacs and Moshes and Samuels were quick to take advantage of the opportunity, the last chance, never quite realizing that all they were accomplishing was the strange metamorphosis of Irving and Morris and Sidney from English to Jewish names.

Joshua Cohen liked his first name. It was his—his father and mother had given it to him and he wanted to keep it. But he had no such feelings toward his surname, which was properly neither his nor his father's. When his father had migrated from Russia the Immigration Officer had stood, pen poised, and asked him what his last name was.

"Schmutschkevitsch," said Joshua's father.

The Immigration Officer didn't make the mistake of attempting to find out or guess how Schmutschkevitsch might be spelled. He asked, instead, where Joshua's father had been born. It was convenient to use the place of birth as a last name, far more convenient than worrying over the possible spelling of Schmutschkevitsch.

"Byessovetrovsk," said Joshua's father. The Immigration Officer, who sincerely wished that all these Russian Jews had had the good sense to be born in Moscow or Kiev or Odessa or something simple like that, closed his eyes for a moment and wiped perspiration from his forehead.

"Your name's Cohen," he declared. "Next!"

When Josh Crawford walked off the little stage in the small auditorium on Hester Street with his diploma in his hand, he felt thoroughly comfortable with his new name. Some of his classmates tried to make him a little less comfortable—it was all well and good to change Isaac to Irving, but the boy who changed Cohen to Crawford was taking a pretty big step. Josh ignored them, and in the fall he registered at Stuyvesant High School as Joshua Crawford and nobody saw anything wrong in the new name.

Even before the graduation ceremonies at PS 105, Joshua Crawford's life was mapped out and set on its course. He would go to Stuyvesant and graduate at or near the top of his class. From there he would move on to City College where Ivy League educations were dispensed at no cost to the recipient.

Meanwhile he would work—afternoons after school, evenings, and Saturdays. His mother would not approve of his working on the Sabbath but this could not be helped, for law school was not tuition-free and he had already decided that he would go to law school immediately upon graduation from CCNY. In order to do this he would have to have money saved up, and in order to save up money he would have to work, and if Sabbath observance had to suffer that was just one of those things. Even at the age of nineteen, Josh Crawford had come to the profound realization that the only way to hold your head up and enjoy life in America was to have as much money as possible. America was filled to overflowing with money and he was out to get his.

He got it. It was not easy and it was not accomplished without work and sacrifice, but Josh was a born worker and a willing sacrificer. He was by no means the smartest boy at Stuyvesant but he finished far ahead of most of the brighter boys. Many of them were dreamers while he was a planner and this made a big difference. He studied what had to be studied and worked over what had to be worked over and his marks were always very high.

He worked afternoons pushing a garment truck on Seventh Avenue for a dress manufacturer who had lived on Essex Street just a block or two away from where Josh was born. The work was hard and the pay was small, but while he did not earn much money he spent hardly any at all. He worked Saturdays wrapping parcels at Gimbel's, and he saved that money, too.

When he went to City as a pre-law major his studies were correspondingly harder and he had to give up the afternoon job. But it didn't matter—by the time he had completed three years at City, he had enough money and enough academic credits to enter law school at New York University.

Law school, clerkship, bar exams, flunkey work. Junior partner, member of the firm.

Hester Street, 14th Street, Central Park West, New Rochelle, Dobbs Ferry.

$15-a-week, $145-a-week, $350-a-month, $9550-a-year, $35,000-a-year.

His life was a series of triumphs, triumphs represented by titles and addresses and numbers. The setbacks, such as they were, were negative rather than positive disappointments. He never failed at anything he set out to do, not in the long run, and his few setbacks were in point of time. If it took him a year longer to become a junior partner, an extra few years to become a member of the firm, if his salary (or, when he was a member of Taylor, Lazarus and Crawford, his average annual income) moved along more slowly than he wished, this was unfortunate but something swiftly corrected.

The apartment on 14th Street was more private and more comfortable than the flat he had shared with his parents on the Lower East Side. The apartment on Central Park West was still more comfortable, as were in turn the house in New Rochelle and the larger and more desirable house in Dobbs Ferry.

Somewhere along the line he got married. Marriage never figured prominently in his plans. After a time it became professionally desirable, and when that happened a marriage broker in the old neighborhood went to work and came up with a wife for him.

The girl, Selma Kaplan, was neither homely nor attractive. Her reasons for marrying Josh paralleled his reasons for marrying her. She was at the perilous age where an unmarried girl was well on her way to becoming an old maid, an altogether unappealing prospect. Joshua Crawford was a young man with all the earmarks of success, a definite "good catch," and as his wife she would have security, respect, and a small place in the sun.

They were married between 14th Street and Central Park West, and a month or so before the junior partnership Selma Crawford was deflowered at a good midtown hotel and broken to saddle during a two-week honeymoon at a run-down resort in the Poconos. She was neither the best nor the worst woman Josh had slept with, just as she was neither the first nor the last, and her general lack of enthusiasm for sexual relations was cancelled out by her lack of distaste for the sex act.

She was a good cook, a good housekeeper, an adequate mother for Lewis and Sybil Crawford. The family's living quarters were never untidy, the cupboard was never bare, and the children grew up without displaying any of the more obvious neuroses that Selma read about periodically in the books that were periodically being read on Central Park West.

Her life was her home, her children, and her female friends who lived lives much the same as her own. Her husband's life was his work, his own advancement in the world, his business acquaintances. If you had asked Selma Crawford whether or not she loved her husband, she would have answered at once that she did; in private she might have puzzled over your question, might have been a bit disturbed by it. If you asked the same question of Josh Crawford he would probably answer in much the same way. He, however, would not puzzle over the question—it would be answered automatically and forgotten just as automatically the minute he had answered it.

Love, all things considered, had nothing to do with it. Joshua and Selma Crawford lived together, brought up children together, worked separately and together to achieve the Great American Dream. They enjoyed what any onlooker would have described as the perfect marriage.

That is, until Josh Crawford did a very strange thing, a thing which he himself was hard put to explain to himself. He might have blamed it on his age—he was forty-six—or on the fact that his professional advancement had more or less leveled off to an even keel. But wherever you place the blame, the action itself stands.

Joshua Crawford fell in love with a young prostitute named Honour Mercy Bane.


"Accredited Paper Goods," said a female voice.

"This is Joshua Crawford."

A pause. A name was checked in a file of 3x5 index cards. Then: "Good afternoon, Mr. Crawford. What can we do for you?"

"I'd like a shipment early this evening, if possible."

"Certainly, Mr. Crawford. We've got a fresh shipment of 50-weight stock that just arrived at the warehouse a week ago. Good material in a red-and-white wrapping."

"Fine," Crawford said.

"You'll want delivery at the usual address?"

"That's right."

"We can have the order to you by nine o'clock," the voice said. "Will that be all right?"

"Fine," said Crawford.

Crawford rang off, then called Selma in Dobbs Ferry and told her he'd be working late at the office. The call completed, he leaned back in his chair and lit a cigarette. The phone call to "Accredited Paper Goods" wasn't particularly subtle, he thought. Fifty-weight stock in a red-and-white wrapping meant a fifty-dollar call girl with red hair and white skin, and by no stretch of the imagination could it have anything in the world to do with paper.

But the subterfuge did have a certain amount of value. It kept any law enforcement personnel from gathering anything other than circumstantial evidence over the phone, and it kept undesirable clients from getting through to the girls. Besides, he thought cynically, the cloak-and-dagger aspect of it all lent a certain air of excitement to the whole routine.

Crawford finished the cigarette and put it out. He was looking forward to the arrival of the shipment. It had been almost two months since he'd had any woman other than his wife and that was a long time, especially in view of the fact that it was a rare night indeed when he and Selma shared the same bed. He wasn't a chaser the way so many of his friends were, didn't want a young thing to make him feel young again, didn't make a habit of seducing his friends' wives or chasing down the young flesh that worked around the office.

He was a man who believed in buying what he wanted, and when he wanted a woman he bought one. The fifty dollars or so that it set him back for a woman was inconsequential to him and, in the long run, far cheaper than wining and dining a girl for the doubtful joy of seducing her free of charge. This way seemed far cleaner to him—you dialed a number, said some crap about a shipment of paper goods, had a good dinner at a good restaurant, and then went to your apartment on East 38th Street.

The apartment, which cost him a little under two hundred

dollars a month, was something which he had to have, anyway. There were enough nights when he had to work late legitimately, sometimes until two or three or even four in the morning before an important case, and at that hour it was a headache to look around for a hotel room and a pain in the ass to drive home to Dobbs Ferry. He'd had the apartment for better than five years now and it was a pleasure to have it, a pleasure to be able to run over there for a nap in the middle of the day if he was tired, and a pleasure to be able to have a girl there every once in a while.

He knocked off work a few minutes before five, had a pair of martinis in the bar across the street with Sid Lazarus, and had a good blood-rare steak and an after-dinner cigar at the steakhouse on the corner of 36th and Madison. One of the junior partners had recently managed to become a father and the cigar was the result of the occasion; it was a damned fine Havana and Crawford smoked it slowly and thoughtfully. He took a long time over dinner and a longer time with the cigar, and it was almost eight-thirty when he took the elevator to the third floor of the apartment house on East 38th Street.

The girl who arrived on the stroke of nine was young and lovely with chestnut hair and a full figure. They had a drink together and then they went to the bedroom where they took off their clothes and slipped into the comfortable double bed and made love all night long.

It had been better in Newport.

The thought was a disloyal one and Honour Mercy took a long look around her own apartment to get the thought out of her head. She and Richie had been sharing the apartment for almost two weeks now and it was a pleasure to look at it. It was easily the nicest place she had ever lived in her life.

Shortly after she and Marie had "gone to see a man about a whore," Honour Mercy had learned that it was unnecessary to live in a rat-trap like the hotel on 47th Street where they had taken a room. The man Marie had taken her to see had decided that Honour Mercy was too damned good-looking to waste her time streetwalking and had put her on call. Since she didn't have to take men to her apartment but went either to theirs, or to a hotel room rented for the occasion, she didn't have to live in the type of hotel that would let her earn her living on the premises. She could live wherever she could afford to live, and after a few days on the job she saw that she could afford to live a good deal better than she was living.

She earned roughly two hundred dollars the first week on the job and close to three hundred the second. If a man wanted her for the afternoon or evening it cost him fifty dollars, if he wanted her for a quickie it cost twenty-five, and half of what she was paid was hers to keep. The organization which employed her took care of everything—she had a phone at the apartment and they called her periodically, telling her just where to go and exactly what to do.

One day she had seven quickies in the course of the afternoon and evening. Another day she was paid to entertain an out-of-town buyer from noon until the following morning, accompanying him and another couple to dinner and a night club. That time she was paid an even hundred dollars. Then, too, there were days when she earned nothing at all, but with her half of the take, plus whatever tip a client wanted to give her, her take-home pay added up to a healthy sum.

As a result, there was no reason in the world for her and Richie to be living on West 47th Street. It took her two days to decide this and a few more days to find the right apartment, but now she was settled in a first-floor three-room apartment in the West Eighties just a few doors from Central Park West. It might be pointed out irrelevantly that her apartment was right around the corner from the apartment in which Joshua and Selma Crawford had first set up housekeeping eighteen years ago.

And it was very nice apartment, she thought. Wall-to-wall carpeting on the floors, good furniture, a tile bathroom, a good-sized kitchen—all in all, it was a fine place to live.

Much better than the Casterbridge Hotel.

She shook her head angrily. Then why in the world did the thought keep creeping into her head that things were a lot better in Newport? It didn't make sense, not with the nicer place she was living in and the nicer money she was earning.

The trouble was, things were so all-fired complicated. In Newport, things couldn't be simpler. You got up and went to Madge's house and went to work. You turned a certain amount of tricks and went home to Richie. You sat around, or maybe went to a movie or spent some time talking to Terri, and then you went to bed with Richie. In the morning you woke up and went to work, or in the evening you woke up and went to work, and either way it was the same every day, with the same place and the same people and the same thoughts in your head.

But not anymore. Now she was working in a different place every day, taking cabs to hotel rooms and apartments, working all different hours. And Richie wasn't at the apartment all the time the way he was always at the hotel room in Newport. You'd think that with a nice apartment to stay in he'd be home all the time, but not Richie. She wondered where he was now, where he'd been spending all his time.

"You got a pimp?" Marie had asked her once. She had told her that she hadn't, and then another time she had mentioned Richie.

"This the guy who's your pimp?"

"No," she said. "I told you I don't have a pimp. He just lives with me."

"He got a job?"

"No."

"He lives on what you make?"

"That's right."

Marie laughed. "Honey," she said, "I don't know where the hell you're from, or what the hell they call it in Newport, but you got a pimp, whether you know it or not."

This sort of talk didn't exactly bolster her morale. Honour Mercy knew what a pimp was, certainly. She knew that almost all the girls in the business had one. But she had never thought of Richie in just those terms. Oh, he fit the definition well enough. She supported him and he didn't do any work at all, didn't even look for work.

But . . .

Well, he *couldn't* work. That was what she told herself, but it was harder to believe it in New York than it had been in Newport. He was about as safe in New York as a needle in a haystack, and no Air Police all the way from Scott Air Force Base were going to chase clear through to New York for him. But he still didn't try to get a job.

She shook her head. No, she had to admit it was more that he didn't want to work. Whenever she brought the subject up, he went into how it wasn't safe, how they had his fingerprints on file and he couldn't make a move without them getting on his trail. Each time he explained it to her, but each time the explanation became just that much less convincing. Why, he could get a job without getting his fingerprints taken. And he could surely be as safe on a job as he could walking all over the city and heaven-knows-what.

She paced around the apartment for a while, sat down, got up and paced some more. A good friend would help, she thought. Somebody like Terri, for instance. For a while she had thought that Marie would take Terri's place, but with Marie being a lesbian, things just didn't work out that way. Whenever she was with Marie, the older woman would want to do things that Honour Mercy didn't want to do, and the situation was strained on both sides. Now she hadn't seen Marie in days and didn't much care if she never saw her again.

She paced some more, sat some more, and started pacing again.

She kept walking and sitting until the phone rang and she was in business again.


While the cab carried her to 171 East 38th Street, she wondered what kind of a man Mr. Crawford was that he wanted her again so soon. He was a very nice man—he tipped her ten dollars both of the times she had visited him at his apartment and never asked her to do anything that she didn't like to do. He was good, too, and when she was with a man all night she had a chance to enjoy it if he was good. Sometimes this made her feel a little disloyal to Richie, but then she would tell herself that this was her work and it was no crime to enjoy your work.

But the thing about Mr. Crawford that she especially liked was that he didn't make her feel bad. And that, when you came right down to it, was what made New York worse than Newport. In Newport you were just with a man for a few minutes and he didn't have a chance to make you feel bad, but in New York you were with a man sometimes for the whole night—and with the out-of-town buyer about twenty hours—and when you were with a man that long, you usually felt bad by the time it was over.

Not from anything the men did. Not from anything they did or said, but from the way they felt toward you and the way you felt toward yourself when you were with them. When you were with a man that long, you couldn't have sex *all* the time, and when you weren't having sex you felt uncomfortable. It was hard to explain but it was there.

That was the good thing about Mr. Crawford. She never had felt uncomfortable with him, not either of those times. The second night she had been so at ease that, when they made love, she just closed her eyes and pretended to herself that she and Mr. Crawford were married. It was funny, and very weird, and afterward she felt guilty, but while they were doing it, it was very good for her, and it was even good afterward when they lay side by side in silence and he looked at her with his eyes gentle and his mouth smiling.

He was waiting for her when she got to the apartment. He opened the door for her, closed it behind her and took her coat. He led her to a chair, handed her a drink, and took a seat in a chair across the room from her.

"It's good to see you," he said. "How have you been, Honey?"

"All right."

"I haven't," he said. "I just lost an important case."

"Oh," she said. "I'm sorry."

"So am I, but I expected it. Damn fool of a client didn't have a leg to stand on, but he insisted on going to court. Some of them are so damned stupid they ought to be shot. They get the idea of suing for a few hundred thousand and the numbers get them intoxicated. They smell money they haven't got a chance in the world of collecting, and the money-smell goes to their heads. I told the damn fool he couldn't collect, but he was determined to go to court. What the hell—I figured we might as well get the fee as some shysters. But it's a pain in the neck, Honey."

"I can imagine."

His face had been very serious and now it relaxed. "By the way," he said, "do you call yourself anything besides Honey? It's a hell of a name."

She told him her name.

"Honour Mercy," he echoed. "I like that. Has a good sound to it. You mind if I call you that instead of Honey?"

"Whatever you want, Mr. Crawford."

He laughed, and after she realized how funny it was to be calling him Mr. Crawford, she laughed too. "My friends call me Josh," he said. "Josh belongs in the same class with Honey as far as I'm concerned. Why don't you try Joshua?"

"Joshua," she said to herself, testing the name.

"The guy who fought the battle of Jericho."

"And the walls came tumbling down."

He nodded. "You know, there's a rational explanation for that whole episode. If you find the right note for a certain object, the right vibration, and sound it long enough, the object'll fall or crack or whatever the hell it does."

She didn't understand, so he went over the explanation in more detail, which wasn't easy because he wasn't too clear on just what he was saying. But they talked about the battle of Jericho, and the Bible in general, and Honour Mercy started suddenly when she realized that she hadn't been thinking of the conversation as part of turning a trick. It was just two people talking, two friendly people in a pleasant apartment, and the real purpose of the visit had gotten lost in the shuffle.

When he had finished talking about vibrations and wave lengths and other sundry physical phenomena, there was a moment of silence and Honour Mercy realized that he couldn't turn the conversation or the mood to sex now, that he was probably a little embarrassed and that it was up to her. She got halfway out of her chair, intending to go to him and embrace him and kiss him, but before she was on her feet he shook his head and she sank back into the chair.

"Let's just talk, Honour Mercy."

She nodded agreeably.

"I mean it," he said. "I just want you to sit here and talk with me. For the moment, anyway."

Normally she would have gone along with him. That was automatic—if a customer was paying for your time and just wanted to talk or watch a floor show or listen to music, that was his business. Marie had told her that quite frequently homosexuals engaged girls for the evening to kill rumors about themselves, that other men actually wanted no more than an evening's companionship exclusive of sex. Already she had met men who liked to build themselves up by talking for hours before getting down to business.

But this time—perhaps the closeness she was beginning to feel for Crawford—made her ask: "Is that what you called me over for? To talk?"

"I don't know."

She looked at him.

"I really don't know," he said. "As a matter of fact, I didn't have anything in mind one way or the other when I called the agency. Neither sex nor conversation. I felt a little disappointed about the case I had been working on and a bit annoyed over things in general and I simply wanted to see you."

"All right."

"I wanted somebody," he said. "Do you have any idea what it's like to want somebody—not anybody specifically, but just somebody to relax with? I wanted to talk to somebody. Who could I talk to? My wife? I haven't talked to her in years, just the usual where-did-you-go-what-did-you-do crap. My partners? With them I could talk law. That's all we have in common—law. My kids? They're good kids, fine kids. I don't know 'em, but they're good kids. If something happened to them it would kill me. I love them. But how in hell could I possibly talk to them? We wouldn't have anything to talk about." She didn't say anything.

"Forty-six years," he said. "Forty-six years and I've done fine not talking to anybody. Forty-six years and I haven't missed it. So this afternoon I felt like talking for maybe the first time in forty-six years, and there wasn't a soul I could talk to. It's a hell of a thing."

He lapsed into silence. She waited a minute and then said: "What do you want to talk about?"

"You talk. I've talked too damned much already."

"What should I talk about?"

"I don't really give a damn," he said. "Talk about whatever the hell you want to talk about. Tell me what you eat for breakfast, or where you get your hair done, or who you like in the fifth at Tropical. I'll just listen."

She wondered what he was driving at. She thought that he was probably making some sort of a pitch, a private speech, a summation to a private jury. But he was a nice man and she liked him and so she started to talk.

She started with her childhood—perhaps because that's an easy place to start, perhaps because coming of age in Coldwater is hardly a controversial topic of conversation. She started there, and before she knew what was happening she was giving him a short history of her life. She talked about Lester Balcom and Madge and Terri and Dee, about Richie and Marie, about the way she felt when she was home alone and the way she felt riding in a cab to an assignation. She needed to talk at least as much as he did and the words poured out of her, and as they did they had a somewhat therapeutic effect upon both of them. Any priest will tell you that confession is good for the soul even if there has been no sin, that the urge to share experience with another human being is a powerful urge that demands satisfaction.

Neither of them kept any track of the time. Finally she had run out of words and the two of them sat quietly and stared thoughtfully at each other. Honour Mercy sipped at her drink and discovered that her glass was empty. Perhaps she had finished it or perhaps it had evaporated; she had no memory of anything but a continual monologue.

Crawford stood up, walked over to her and looked down at her. He reached into his pocket and took out two bills, a fifty and a ten. He handed them to her.

"Go on home," he told her.

She handed the money back to him. "You can't pay me until I earn it."

"You've earned it. More than earned it."

"Joshua—"

He smiled when she said his name. "I mean it," he said. "I don't want to . . . sleep with you. Not now."

"Because you're paying for it?"

He didn't say anything.

"You listen to me now," she said. "You're going to take this money and put it back in your pocket. Then you and me are going back in that bedroom and we're going to bed together. And when we're done you're not giving me any money because I'm not going to let you. You understand?"

"Don't be silly."

"I'm not being silly."

"Look—"

She stood up and looked straight into his eyes. He had very dark brown eyes that were almost black in the artificial light of the room. "You wanted me to talk to you," she said. "I liked you and so I talked to you. I told you a lot of things I never told to anybody else."

"I know."

"I told you because I like you. And now I want you to go to bed with me. Don't you like me enough to do that?"

He didn't say anything.

"Take my arm, Joshua."

He took her arm.

"Now . . . now lead me to the bedroom. And afterwards don't you dare to try to give me money or I'll hate you. Maybe I won't hate you but I'll be mad. I mean it."

He took her into the bedroom and put on the small lamp and closed the door. He stood motionless by the side of the bed until she had removed her dress; then he too started to disrobe.

When they were both nude they turned to look at each other. He looked at full thighs and a narrow waist and firm breasts; she looked at a body that was still youthful, at a chest matted with dark curly hair.

He didn't move. She stepped close to him and her arms went around his body.

She said: "Please kiss me, Joshua."

# CHAPTER 6

The bartender, standing down at the end of the bar, looked at Richie and obviously didn't much care for what he saw. Richie was impaled by the look; he squirmed on it, his face got red, his eyes dropped. He knew what was coming.

With an exaggerated air of Job-like long-suffering, the bartender pushed himself off his elbow and came dirty-aproned strolling down the length of the bar. Stopping in front of Richie, he said, in a weary voice, "How old are you, kid?"

Richie met the barman's eyes for just a second. In Richie's eyes was pleading, in the barman's implacability. Without a word, Richie slid off the stool and skulked, round-shouldered, back to the cold and sunlit street. He turned left, aimlessly, and walked along with his hands in his pockets, imagining himself, after an extensive course in judo, coming back and drop-kicking that bartender through his back-mirror.

The hell of it was, Richie was eighteen. And eighteen was legal drinking age in New York State.

But he just didn't look eighteen. He was short and skinny to begin with, and that didn't help. His face was weak and watery, and that didn't help. And he'd been living soft. He'd put on over twenty pounds, and he'd spouted acne instead of whiskers, and *that* didn't help. The twenty pounds didn't make him look less skinny. It just made him look like a skinny sixteen-year-old with baby fat on his cheeks.

Nine chances out of ten, he could have shown his Air Force ID card (being on active duty, he had no draft card) and been served without question. But he was terrified to show that card anywhere, just as he was honestly terrified to try to get a job or to open a bank account (assuming he had money to put in it) or get to know anybody besides Honour Mercy. Richie Parsons' concept of Authority was basically the same as George Orwell's in *1984*. Authority was a Big Brother, mysteriously everywhere, all-knowing and all-seeing, waiting to pounce upon Richie Parsons the second he made a mistake, and bear him whimpering back to Scott Air Force Base, where the whole squadron would line up to kick the shit out of him, and then he'd probably go to Leavenworth or something.

The days, for Richie Parsons, were long and empty. And the nights were even longer. Staying in the apartment all the time, waiting for a Knock On The Door, was too much for his nerves to stand. And Honour Mercy was practically never at home. Her work now took her away, usually, in the early evening, and she was never back before two or three in the morning, and sometimes she wasn't back until long after sun-up. She'd even been away over a whole weekend once, off on somebody's yacht, she and a number of her coworkers, with a group of rich college boys and a photographer from a men's magazine. That was only two weeks ago, and Honour Mercy was already haunting the newsstands, wondering if they'd used a picture of her. "They probably won't, though," she kept saying. "The only picture he took of me was one I don't think they could use."

The point was that Richie was most of the time alone. Honour Mercy was the only one he knew that he could freely associate with, and she was usually either working or sleeping.

Besides that, Honour Mercy seemed to be changing. Her attitude toward Richie was undergoing a very uncomfortable transformation. She was talking more and more frequently, lately, about the fact that Richie wasn't working. She was even beginning to nag a little about it, as though he could safely go off and get a job somewhere, when he knew without question that it was too dangerous to even think about.

Honour Mercy was changing in other ways, too. Sometimes, her customers would take her out to dinner or a show or something first, and Honour Mercy had by now seen most of the Broadway shows and been to a lot of the midtown nightclubs. She was learning to dress like the ads in the fashion magazines (though nothing in the world could shrink her bust to fashionable boyishness), and a faint southern-ness in her speech was rapidly disappearing. She was, in a word, becoming sophisticated, and she and Richie no longer had quite so much in common.

It was a problem, and Richie gnawed worriedly at it as he wandered down the street from the bar where he hadn't been served. Life had been comparatively sweet for him the last couple of months. With neither the cloying demands of his mother or the harsh demands of the Air Force to contend with, he could live at his own slow pace. He had no duties, no responsibilities. But now, with Honour Mercy on the one hand growing away from him, and on the other hand becoming more insistent that he should find a job, life was getting complicated again, and Richie, as usual, didn't have the foggiest idea what to do about it.

He was walking east on 77th Street, toward the park. Central Park West was straight ahead, at the end of a row of brownstones. When he got to the corner, he hesitated, wondering where to go next. The park was loaded with frantic, round-eyed boys who kept trying to pick him up, and that made him nervous. To the right was midtown, where he could probably find a bar that would serve him if he looked long enough and hard enough. To the left was home, eight blocks away, but this was Thursday afternoon and Honour Mercy would be at the hairdresser's.

He wanted something to drink, but he didn't feel like braving the histrionic weariness of any more bartenders. On the other hand, he could buy a six-pack of beer in any grocery store, take it home, and wait for Honour Mercy to come back.

All right, that's what he'd do. He walked uptown, on the side away from the park, and turned left at 85th Street. The apartment was in the middle of the block, and a tiny grocery store was two doors farther down. He walked slowly, having nothing in the world to hurry for, and when someone said his name as he was passing his building, he almost fainted.

He froze. He stood still, staring down the empty sidewalk toward Columbus Avenue, and the voice ran round and round inside his head. "Richie Parsons?" A strange voice, one he'd never heard before, and there had been a questioning lilt on the last syllable.

It was Authority. It had to be, nobody knew him here, nobody wanted to know him. He froze, and wished desperately to disappear.

The voice repeated his name, still with the rising inflection, and Richie forced himself to turn and look at the Authority that had descended upon him.

But it didn't seem to be Authority after all. There was a black Lincoln parked at the curb in front of the building, and there was a man in the driver's seat, looking out at Richie. He was middle-aged, black-haired, with dark and deep-set eyes, a thin-lipped wide mouth and a heavily lined face. He seemed Stern and he seemed Successful and he was obviously Rich, but he didn't look like Authority.

He didn't look like Authority because his expression was one of polite curiosity, the expression of a man who has asked a not-too-important question and is waiting for the not-too-important answer. Such was not the expression of Authority.

Richie hesitated, wondering what to answer. Should he deny the name, go on down to the corner, go to a movie, wait until this man had given up and gone away? Or should he admit that he was, in fact and in essence, Richie Parsons?

The man had called him by name. He could have gotten the name only from one of two sources: Honour Mercy or Authority. The latter, despite his expression, seemed the most likely. Authority, in a Chinese-eyed Lincoln?

The man broke into his hesitation by smiling and saying, "Don't worry, Richie. I'm not the law. I'm a friend of Honour Mercy's."

"Honour Mercy?" he echoed. He was at a complete loss.

"Hop in," said the man. "I want to talk to you."

"Talk to me?" When Richie was confused, more than usually confused, he was in the habit of repeating what was said to him, turning it into a question.

"Don't worry," said the man. "I'm not going to turn you over to the Air Force."

Richie stared at him, and fought down the urge to say, "Air Force?" Instead, he said, "How do you know about it?"

"Honour Mercy told me. Come on, hop in. I'll explain the whole thing."

Richie couldn't think of anything else to do, so he hopped in. He walked around the Mandarin front of the Lincoln, opened the shiny black door, and sat tentatively on the maroon upholstery.

The man immediately started the engine, which purred at the lowest threshold of audibility, and the Lincoln pulled smoothly away from the curb.

For the first part of the ride, the man was silent, and Richie followed his example. They went directly across town first, and up a ramp to the Henry Hudson Parkway, where the speedometer needle moved up to fifty and hovered, while the city rolled by to the left, and the Hudson became the ocean to the right. They dipped into the Brooklyn Battery tunnel, emerged on the Brooklyn side, and headed almost due east.

Brooklyn was, as usual, snarled with traffic. Their ride was hyphenated by red lights, and the man began to talk. "My name is Joshua Crawford," he said. "I'm forty-six years of age, I've got two children, both of them older than you, I'm a well-to-do lawyer, and I've believed in the straight-forward approach all of my life. I want you to know this about me, I want you to know anything you want about me. For two reasons. First, I know at least as much about you. Second, I want you to have the full facts in the case before you make your decision."

"My decision?" Richie was confused again.

"Just hear me out," said Joshua Crawford. "I've known Honour Mercy now for about two months. You might say we were business acquaintances. Her business, not mine. Something—I'm not sure what—made me think of Honour in an unbusiness-like way. Don't get me wrong; I don't make a habit of befriending whores. This time, something is different. I can't define it any closer than that."

A traffic light ahead of them switched from green through orange to red, and the purring Lincoln stopped. Joshua Crawford looked over at Richie Parsons. "Has Honour Mercy mentioned me at all?" he asked.

"No," said Richie. "She doesn't tell me much about her—about her work."

"Good," said Crawford. "That's just another example of how she's different. Practically any whore, if she gets a steady customer, and she and the customer are friends, she'll go around boasting about it. Honour Mercy's different. She isn't a whore by nature. She shouldn't be in such a business."

His words hung in the air between them, the light switched back to green, and the Lincoln nosed forward again.

"I want to help Honour Mercy," said Crawford after a minute. "I want to put her into what might be called semi-retirement."

"Your mistress," said Richie, beginning to understand at last what this was all about.

Crawford nodded without taking his eyes away from the traffic-filled street. "My mistress," he said. "I have plans for Honour Mercy. A good apartment—better than where she is now. Money of her own, charge accounts at a couple of the better stores. She would, in every sense but the legal, be my wife. There's a woman out in Dobbs Ferry who is my wife in the legal sense, and that's all."

While Richie waited for what he knew was coming next, Crawford spun the wheel and the Lincoln made a right turn. They were on a wider street now, with less traffic, and the speedometer needle inched upward again.

"I have plans for Honour Mercy," repeated Crawford. "But you don't fit into those plans. You were apparently willing to share the girl with all takers. I'm not willing to share her with anybody."

Richie nodded, and a lost and helpless feeling was beginning to spread over him, and he wondered, with a vague fear, what Joshua Crawford's plans were for Richie Parsons.

"We're in competition, you and I," continued Crawford. "Ridiculous, but true. And I think you'll have to agree with me that there's no contest."

The silence lengthened again, and Richie realized he was expected to make some sort of answer. At last he mumbled, "I suppose so."

"The easy thing for me to do," said Crawford, "was let the police know where you were. Easy. But also cruel and unnecessary. I'm not a cruel man, Richie, and I don't do the unnecessary. So I'm giving you your choice."

"What choice?" asked Richie miserably. He could see no choice.

Crawford took one hand from the steering wheel long enough to reach within the jacket of his tailored suit and withdraw a business-size envelope. He dropped the envelope on the seat between them. "It's getting cold in New York," he said. "Winter is on the way, and you're going to have to start shifting for yourself. There's a one-way plane ticket to Miami in that envelope, plus five hundred dollars in ten-dollar bills. Enough to keep you alive until you find a place for yourself down there. You can take the ticket and the money and go to Miami, and that's the end of it. Or you can decide to stay."

Richie knew that he was now supposed to ask what would happen if he were to decide to stay, and he also knew what the answer would be. But he was supposed to ask, and he did. "What if I don't go?"

"I call the police," said Crawford, "and you go back to Scott Air Force Base."

Richie looked gloomily out the window. He saw a street sign, and saw that they were now traveling on Rockaway Parkway, and it seemed to him that it shouldn't be "Parkaway, we'll rock away together."

He parked his thoughts back where they belonged. Joshua Crawford was driving him to the airport, that was clear enough. He had to decide, he had to make up his mind what to do.

But what decision was there? Take the ticket and the money, take the plane, go away to Miami and see what would happen next. Or stay here and be taken by the police. What choice was that?

A sudden thought came to him, and he voiced it. "What does Honour Mercy say?"

"I haven't said anything to her yet," said Crawford. "I want you out of the way first."

"How do you know she'll become your mistress?"

"She will," said Crawford. "If you aren't around. And you won't be around, one way or the other."

Richie leaned against the door on his side and gnawed on his lower lip, sinking easily into depression and self-pity. He compared himself with Joshua Crawford, and he found himself coming in a very distant second. Joshua was rich, he was successful, he was assured, he was strong. He was driving this car, he could give Honour Mercy anything she wanted. Richie Parsons was young, he was poor and uncertain and weak and afraid. He could give Honour Mercy nothing but himself, and that was a poor gift indeed.

"What's your choice?" Crawford asked him.

Wordlessly, Richie reached out and picked up the envelope.

"You understand," said Crawford, "that this is permanent. If you try to get in touch with either Honour Mercy or myself, I'll have to turn you in. You understand that?"

"Yes," whispered Richie.

Somewhere, they crossed the line separating Brooklyn from Queens, and wound up on a divided highway, and the speedometer needle moved up to sixty. Then they turned off the highway to another highway and signs said that they were entering New York International Airport, known as Idlewild.

Idlewild was as big as Scott Air Force Base, which meant it was larger than any airport should be. There was a four-lane divided highway within the airport grounds, and sprawling low buildings far off the highway on either side bore huge signs giving the names of various airlines.

The temporary terminal was miles away from the main entrance, but finally they got to it and the Lincoln slowed to a stop.

"Here we are," said Crawford. He looked at Richie and his expression was now sympathetic. "I'm sorry," he said. "But I think this is the best way to do it. For everybody concerned."

Richie mumbled something and got out of the car. Then, all at once, he remembered his uniform, still packed away in the AWOL bag and in the closet at the apartment he'd been sharing with Honour Mercy. "My—my clothes," he said. He was poised half-in and half-out of the car. "I've got to get my clothes."

"Buy some more," said Crawford. His hand dipped down, came up with a wallet, six twenty-dollar bills were suddenly in Richie's hand. "Buy some more," Crawford repeated. "Your plane is leaving at six, and it's after four now."

"But I need—" He couldn't come out and say it, about the uniform.

Crawford was impatient now. He'd obviously thought the whole distasteful thing was over with. "Is there something special you need?"

"Yes."

"What?"

"My—my uniform."

Crawford looked puzzled, and then surprised, and then he smiled. "You're smarter than I gave you credit for," he said. "My apologies. The old deserter dodge, is that it?"

Richie was humiliated and defeated. He mumbled and nodded his head.

"I'll mail it to you," he said. "General Post Office, Miami. You'll have it within the week."

"I need it," said Richie desperately.

"Don't worry; I'll send it to you."

There was nothing Richie could say, nothing he could do. He stepped out onto the concrete, and the door swung shut behind him. He turned to say something—goodbye, something—but the Lincoln was already purring away. He watched it pull out to the main airport road and swing away, back to the city again.

The envelope was cold and crisp in his hand. Holding it tightly, he went into the terminal building and searched for the men's room. Finding it, he invested a coin in privacy, and, once within the stall, opened the envelope. It contained the ticket, one-way, and some ten-dollar bills, fifty of them. With the money Crawford had just handed him, he now had six hundred and twenty dollars. And the ticket.

He'd been bought out, paid off, patted on the head and sent on his way. Never before in his life had he felt quite as weak and puny as he did this minute. He was the ninety-seven-pound weakling from the ads; but in his case the condition was worse. He wasn't merely weak physically. He was weak in every way. He had no force, no stamina, no courage. He could stand up to no one. Crawford had bought him, paid him off—

A sudden thought came to him. Crawford had paid him off. *Why?* Crawford had waited until he was out of the way before approaching Honour Mercy. *Why?* Crawford hadn't taken the easy and simple and inexpensive method of turning Richie over to the Authorities. *Why not?*

There was only one possible reason. Richie was more competition for Crawford than he had supposed, or than Crawford had admitted. There was no other explanation for Crawford's actions.

He thought about the relationship between himself and Honour Mercy, of their meeting in Newport, of her unquestioning acceptance of him, of her no-strings-attached sharing of his lot with him. He remembered how readily she had left Newport with him, willing to go anywhere with him, to leave a steady income and a comparably good life because *he* was in trouble.

Lately, she'd been growing away from him, she'd been talking as though only laziness was keeping him from working and supporting himself. But still they lived together, still they shared the same bed and gave him freely of her money. Still, when they were in bed together, they made love and enjoyed each other as much as ever.

What if Crawford had gone straight to Honour Mercy and given her the choice? Which way would she have gone? Richie had supposed, for a few traitorous moments, that she would naturally go to the stronger and abler and richer man, the man who could offer her the most. But now, when he stopped to think about it, it was obvious that Crawford didn't think that way. Crawford saw little Richie Parsons as a serious threat. And Crawford might be absolutely right.

That was why Crawford had taken this expensive and roundabout method of getting rid of Richie Parsons. If he had reported Richie to the Authorities, and Honour Mercy had found out who had turned Richie in, she would probably have had nothing at all to do with Crawford.

Of course. Crawford himself had said that he did nothing unnecessary, and only if Richie was a strong competitor for the affections of Honour Mercy was this expense of time and money necessary.

Having gone that far, Richie was stopped again. Because there was nothing he could do about it.

If he didn't take the plane, if he went back to Honour Mercy, Crawford would turn him in. There wasn't any doubt of that. If he went back to Honour Mercy, and Honour Mercy chose him over Crawford, Crawford could lose nothing by reporting Richie. But he could gain quite bit. He could gain revenge against Richie for having double-crossed the line.

So there still wasn't any choice. He still had to take that plane at six o'clock.

Richie felt miserable. This was the story of his life. The strong came along and took from him whatever they wanted for themselves, and there was nothing he could do about it. He could sneak around and take bits and pieces from others, coins and watches and wallets left carelessly where he could get his hands on them, but it wasn't the same thing. He couldn't go boldly up to anybody and take what he wanted. Yet other people could do that to him whenever they wanted. They could do it, and they did.

If only he didn't have to be afraid all the time. If only he *could* go out and get a job, any job, just so he wouldn't have to be living on Honour Mercy all the time. If only he could live without being terrified of Authority.

He had to think about it, he had to think this out carefully. He sat in the stall in the men's room at the temporary terminal, Idlewild, Queens, New York City, fifteen miles from Honour Mercy Bane, and he tried to think of something to make the inevitability of her loss less inevitable.

If he had some sort of phony identification card— But still, his fingerprints were on file in Washington. If his fingerprints were ever taken—

For what? Why would anybody take his fingerprints? They

don't take your fingerprints when you just get a simple job somewhere. All he'd need would be false identification of some sort.

If he could steal a wallet— No, that wouldn't be any good, he'd have to steal a wallet from somebody his age and his size and his hair-color and everything else. He needed identification that was clearly *his*. Besides, stolen identification would be just as bad as real identification.

There was a place where he might be able to get a fake identification card. Fake draft card, Social Security card, driver's license, everything. It was a place he'd heard about when he was in high school, a bar you went to and the bartender, if you looked all right, he would pass you on to the guy who could give you the identification. The only trouble was, the place was in Albany, where Richie's home was, and where the police would be most on the lookout for him.

Still, if he wanted to keep Honour Mercy, he had to have fake identification, he had to be able to work, he had to get free of this fear of Authority. If he wanted Honour Mercy badly enough, he would go to Albany and get the fake identification.

But, by the time he came back, Honour Mercy would have gone off with Crawford already, and he wouldn't know where to look for her. Besides, false identification cost a lot of money.

He had a lot of money. He had six hundred and twenty dollars. He had a ticket to Miami, and he could turn that in for more money. And he didn't have to come back for Honour Mercy; he could bring her along with him.

Of course. That would be a lot safer, anyway. The Albany police would be looking for Richie Parsons, but they wouldn't be looking for him with a girl. They'd be looking for him alone.

And if he took Honour Mercy away with him, then Crawford couldn't get her.

He hurried from the men's room, searching for a phone booth, finally found one, and dialed home. It was quarter-past-four, according to the clock high on the terminal wall. Crawford had started back only fifteen minutes ago, and it would take him an hour at least to get to the apartment. If Honour Mercy were home—

She was. "It's me," Richie said, when she answered the phone. "It's me. Richie."

"Where are you?" she asked. "You sound as though you've been running."

He was on the verge of telling her the whole story, but instinctive caution stopped him. Crawford thought Richie was dangerous competition. Richie was inclined to agree with him. But something told him not to chance putting it to the test. Instead of telling her the truth, therefore, he said, "Something's happened. We've got to get out of New York."

"Right now?"

"Right away. We can go to Albany. I can get some phony identification cards there, and then we'll be all right."

"I thought you didn't want to go to Albany."

She was right. He didn't. The idea of it made him weak. But if he wanted Honour Mercy, he had to do it. And he wanted Honour Mercy. "I'll explain when I see you," he said. "Pack everything right away. I'll meet you at Grand Central Station. By the—by the Information booth. Get two tickets to Albany. I'll be there as soon as I can. An hour, maybe less."

"What happened, Richie?"

"I'll explain when I get there," he said, and hung up before she could ask any more.

It took five long minutes to turn the ticket in for cash, filling out some silly form about why he wasn't going after all, and then he ran out of the terminal and to the nearest taxi-stand. He climbed into the back seat of the cab and said, breathlessly, "Grand Central Station."

The driver looked at him doubtfully. "That's going to cost quite a bit, buddy."

He had six hundred and twenty dollars. He had forty dollars and ninety-two cents for the ticket to Miami. And he was going to stay with Honour Mercy. "I've got the money," he said, and the expansive smile was a new expression on his face. "Don't you worry about it."

CHAPTER 7

Joshua Crawford was sitting with a phone in his hand. The line was dead but he had not yet replaced the receiver. He was staring at a spot on the far wall and his fingers were clenched tight around the receiver.

After a moment he finally did hang up. But he remained in the same position, propped up in front of his desk by his elbows, his eyes still focused absently on the spot on the far wall.

He thought about the conversation. It had been an interesting conversation, to say the least. Almost a fascinating conversation.

It had gone something like this:

"Joshua, this is Honour Mercy. I'm afraid I won't be able to see you tonight."

"Really? What's the matter?"

"I just got a call from Richie."

Guardedly: "Oh?"

"We have to leave town right away. We're catching a train for Albany."

"I see. How come?"

A moment's pause. Then: "He wouldn't tell me. He said something about getting false identification there. I don't know. I think he's afraid the Air Force is after him."

"Is he with you now?"

"No, I'm supposed to meet him right away at Grand Central Station. I have to go now, Joshua. I wanted to call you, though, so you wouldn't worry when I didn't come tonight."

"Well. Thanks for calling."

And that had been that.

The question, Joshua Crawford thought, was just where you went from here. His first reaction, one of cold fury for the little pipsqueak who had the colossal nerve to take his money and use it against him, changed to somewhat renewed respect crossed with determination. The little punk had guts, albeit his own brand of guts. He was putting up a fight, and whether or not that fight consisted of sticking a knife into an obliging back didn't appear to be too relevant.

Whatever way you looked at it, Joshua Crawford was damned lucky. Because this fool Parsons hadn't had the brains to tell her not to, Honour Mercy had given him a more or less complete run-down on their plans. Evidently, Parsons wasn't sure enough of himself to let Honour Mercy know just what was coming off, and this was just fine with Joshua Crawford. The ball had been handed to him; now it was up to him to decide where to throw it.

He toyed with the idea of tipping off the Air Police. The Air Police were, he knew, a most efficient group of gentlemen. In addition to catching Richie as soon as they heard about him, they were almost certain to kick the crap out of him before turning him in. Which, when Joshua Crawford gave the matter a little thought, was just what the little son-of-a-bitch had coming to him. A fast arrest, and a good beating, and as long a sentence in the stockade as they were handing out these days, and Richie

Parsons would disappear from his life like a pesty fly stuck on a ribbon of flypaper.

Crawford hadn't even thought about it before, about what to do if Richie crossed him. The possibility hadn't even occurred to him. Richie, a skulking sneak, a cowardly clod, would take the cash and run like the devil. Period. But things weren't that simple.

Crawford thought about calling the Air Police, thought about Honour Mercy's instant and obvious and inevitable interpretation of such a move, and tried to put himself in her place. If *he* were Honour Mercy, and if some son-of-a-bitch hollered copper on *his* own true love, he would be somewhat annoyed.

It stood to reason that Honour Mercy would react along similar lines.

This more or less ruled out the Air Police. Crawford sat at his desk, thinking, growing even more annoyed. He was beginning to realize that he had blundered, had perhaps done a seriously stupid thing. Everything had been going his way: Honour Mercy and Joshua Crawford were growing more and more together, Honour Mercy and Richie Parsons were sliding further and further apart. In time, with Honour Mercy seeing him constantly and discovering how much more enjoyable his companionship was than Richie's, the battle would have been won.

But he had been too impatient, and in this case impatience and stupidity were identical. He couldn't leave well enough alone—he was like a lawyer with a safe case who tries to bribe the judge for a dismissal instead of waiting for the jury to exonerate his client legally. By rushing things, by being a stupid man, he had forced Honour Mercy and Richie closer together.

Now, he realized, the question had been put. If Richie had a source of false identification papers in Albany, then he no longer had to fear Joshua Crawford, no longer had to be quite so much of a sneak. He would be in a position to offer serious competition to Crawford. It was, all in all, one hell of a mess.

Crawford sat and thought and smoked. The ashtray overflowed and he was developing a callus on his rear from sitting and doing nothing.

There wasn't one hell of a lot he could do. That was the sad part, and it was very sad, but the fact remained that there wasn't a hell of a lot he could do.

He could forget Honour Mercy Bane.

Sure, that's what he could do. He could forget all about her, forget what she was like in bed, what she was like walking and talking and sitting and simply doing nothing but look beautiful. He could forget how he felt alive when he was with her and dead when he was without her.

He could forget her, just as he could forget his name, just as he could remember that he was married to a slob named Selma, just as he could forget that he was alive.

Or, damn it to deep hell, he could get rid of Richie Parsons.

Get rid of him. Get rid of him because he was in the way, because he was an infernal fool who did not fit in with Joshua Crawford's plans. Get rid of him, squash him like the insect he was, use him up and throw him away like a discarded sanitary napkin. The image, he had to admit, was a damned good one.

Get rid of him. Who would miss Richie Parsons? Who could feel anything for him other than a mixture of compassion and contempt?

Joshua Crawford thought some more, then opened his desk

drawer and hunted around for a small book of telephone numbers. Acme Paper Goods was listed in that book, as was Honour Mercy's home phone and a good many other numbers that didn't belong in the official business telephone book. The number Joshua Crawford was looking for was the number of a man named Vincent Canelli. He found the number and dialed it, remembering who Canelli was and what Canelli had said.

Canelli had come to him once, years ago. Canelli did something, God knew what, and Canelli had some sort of mob connection. Along with whatever illegitimate racket the man ran, he also had a dry-cleaning route business that was having hearty tax problems. Crawford had saved the day for him, partly by legal means, partly by reaching people whom Canelli could not have reached on his own.

Canelli had paid a fat fee, which was fitting and proper, but Canelli had also said something else in parting. "Josh," he had said, "you're a right guy. Anything has to be done sometime, you let me know. The way I figure it you got a favor coming. You want a man killed, you just let me know."

The phone was answered on the second ring. Joshua asked for Canelli.

"Who wants him?"

"Joshua Crawford," he told the man, wondering whether Canelli would remember him. Canelli, as it turned out, remembered him perfectly.

He asked if the offer was still good.

"Your phone clear?" Canelli wanted to know. "This line's safe. You sure yours ain't tapped?"

"It's okay, Vince."

"Right. We still better keep it sort of up in the air. Even the telephones have ears. I make it you want to order a hit. Right?"

"Right."

"Here in town?"

Crawford thought for a minute. "No," he said. "Upstate. Albany."

Canelli whistled. "I know people in Albany," he said. "Not too many, but enough. You got somebody to finger the mark?"

The conversation was a little too far up in the air and Crawford had to ask for a translation of the question. "Somebody to point out the prospect so that we make sure we contact the right man," was how it came out the second time around.

"Oh," Crawford said. "Well, no."

"You got his address?"

Crawford thought again. He did not know where Richie would be staying, and he did not know what name Richie would be using, and all in all he did not know one hell of a lot. He considered giving Vince a description, having him meet the train, but he realized that if there was one distinguishing characteristic about Richie Parsons, the insect, it was the utter impossibility of describing him.

"Vince," he said finally, "I guess it won't work. I can't give you enough."

"It's rough without a finger, Josh."

"Yes," Crawford said. "I can understand that."

"If he makes it back to the city—"

"Right," Crawford finished. "I can always call you. In the meantime forget I ever did, okay?"

A low laugh came over the wire. "Josh," Canelli was saying,

"I ain't seen you or heard from you in . . . hell, it must be three years."

"Fine," Crawford said. And, as an afterthought, "How's business?"

"Legit," Canelli told him. "Mostly."

It is no particular problem to get from New York to Albany. The state capital is located approximately one hundred miles due north of the only worthwhile city in the state, and train service between the two points is frequent and excellent. There are a whole host of milk trains departing every few minutes from Grand Central, as well as a bevy of long-haul passenger trains that make Albany the first hitch of a journey that starts from New York and ends up anywhere from Saint Louis to Detroit.

Richie Parsons and Honour Mercy Bane took the Ohio State Limited. The train's ultimate destination was Cincinnati, and it planned on getting there via the indirect route which included Dayton, Springfield, Cincinnati, Buffalo, and, happily, Albany.

Richie and Honour Mercy were on the train when it pulled out of Grand Central at a quarter to six. They were also on the train when it pulled into the Albany terminal at 7:30. The hour and forty-five minutes of monotony which they spent on the train was uneventful, which was just as well as far as Honour Mercy and Richie were concerned. Excitement was the last thing they craved at this point.

"A guy asked me for my draft card," Richie had explained. "He gave me a funny look when I said I left it in my other pants. If he was a cop it would of been all over."

Honour Mercy had nodded sympathetically, but Richie had the feeling that the lie needed a certain amount of embellishing. "So I kept walking," he elaborated. "And I get a few blocks away and I take a quick look over my shoulder, sort of casual-like, and I see the guy. He was trying to be real cool about it but I could tell he was following me."

The additional trappings were obviously just what the lie had needed. Honour Mercy caught her breath and looked worried. Richie had to think for a minute to be sure that it really was a lie, that there hadn't been anybody following him, that no one had asked for his draft card.

"I lost him," he went on. "Leastwise I think I lost him, but maybe he just passed me on to somebody else. I read about how they do it. When one of them gets spotted he signals another one and the other one takes out after you. I looked hard but I couldn't see any other one following me so I guess I got clear."

"It's good you called me," Honour Mercy said. "We have to stay out of town until you have some identification." She was about to tell him that she had called Crawford but she decided not to. He might be jealous, and she didn't want that to happen. It was all perfectly natural discussing Richie with Crawford—he was the kind of man who could listen calmly to anything she said. He understood things. But for some reason it was not perfectly natural to discuss Crawford with Richie.

The private compartment on the train had been Richie's idea. It cost a little more but it was worth it for two reasons. First of all, it was a safety measure—there was no telling when somebody would recognize him, somebody who had known him before. Secondly, it made it look as though he was really worried about being discovered. By this time it was his own private conviction that a visit from the Air Police was about as pressing a danger as an atomic attack on south-central Kansas, but there was no point in letting Honour Mercy in on the fact.

The private compartment, however, accomplished something else. It left Honour Mercy and Richie thoroughly alone with each other, more alone than they had been in quite some time. There they were, the two of them, and with the compartment all closed up they were alone. The togetherness and the aloneness, combined with the marvelous feeling of security that was bound up in the whole idea of false identification papers and the false new identity they would bring, made Richie suddenly very strong, very much the dominant personality. He took Honour Mercy on his lap, and he held Honour Mercy close to him and kissed her, and after he had kissed her several times and touched her breasts, he wished fervently that the trip was over already and they were in a hotel room in Albany.

Which, before too long, is where they were.

From the terminal they taxied to the Conning Towers on State Street. The Conning Towers was, and had been for more years than Richie had been alive, Albany's finest hotel. He had never so much as stepped into the lobby before. It was hardly the most inconspicuous place in town, but Richie reasoned this way: the better the place they stayed in, and the nicer the restaurants they ate in, and the more exclusive neighborhood they roamed around in, the less chance he stood of running into anybody who had known him before.

He figured this out, and he had explained it to Honour Mercy on the train. Even so, he had a tough time telling the cab driver where he wanted to go, and a tougher time actually squaring his shoulders and walking into the lobby. Once inside it was even worse. The high ceilings and the thick carpet made him more nervous, and his voice squeaked when he asked the thin gray clerk for a double room.

The clerk nodded and handed him the register and a ballpoint pen. Richie got enough control over his fingers to get a tentative grip on the pen and leaned over the register to sign his name.

He almost wrote RICHIE PARSONS. The pen was actually touching the paper, ready to make the first stroke of the "R," when it occurred to him that he was no longer Richie Parsons, not if he wanted to stay alive and free. His hand shook and the pen dribbled from his grasp and bounced onto the floor. He reached over to pick it up, hating himself, hating the thin gray clerk, hating everything, and suddenly incapable of thinking up a name for himself.

Then, the pen recovered and poised once more, he remembered the author of a book he had been reading the day before and signed the register ANDREW SHAW. The clerk nodded, attempted a smile, and rang for a bellhop. The bellhop picked up the suitcase that Honour Mercy had packed and led them up an impressively winding staircase to their room on the first floor. The bellhop opened the door, ushered them inside, took an idiotically long time opening the window and checking for soap and towels, and finally accepted the quarter that Richie barely remembered to hand him. Then, mercifully, the bellhop left and closed the door after him.

Only then did Richie relax. He relaxed quite visibly, throwing himself down on the big double bed and letting out his breath all at once.

"Well," Honour Mercy said, "I guess we got here all right."

"I almost ruined everything down there. Signing the book, I mean."

"That's all right," she told him.

"He must figure it's not my name, the way I had so much trouble getting it written."

"Sure," she said, smiling. "He probably thinks you signed another name because we aren't married and you're embarrassed. It's better that way. Surest way in the world to hide something is to pretend you're hiding something else."

Richie thought about that. It made a lot of sense, especially in view of the fact that he had adopted much the same tactics in getting Honour Mercy and himself the hell out of New York. The only difference was that he had hidden what he was running from by pretending to be running from something else, but it worked out to about the same.

"Andrew Shaw," he said aloud, testing the name. "Sounds okay to me. Maybe you ought to practice calling me Andy."

She said *Andy* twice, then laughed. "Sounds funny," she complained. "Can't I call you Richie any more?"

"Not in public. Not when we're out where people can hear and get suspicious."

"How about in private?"

"That's different," he said. He watched her, moving about and unpacking things and putting them away, and he thought that it was time for him to get out of the hotel and get in touch with the man who could fix up the phony identification for him. He watched her some more, watched the way her body moved and studied the way it was formed, and he decided that although it was definitely time to get in touch with the man, the man would be around for a few more hours.

"In bed," he said. "In bed you can call me Richie. When you're in bed with me."

She turned and looked at him. "You want me now?"

He nodded.

"Now?"

"Now."

She started to come toward the bed and he stood up to take her into his arms. When he kissed her he sensed something that he couldn't pin down, some uncertainty or anxiety, but he didn't care to spend any time analyzing it. Anyway, it was gone when he kissed her a second time, and during the third kiss when they were lying together on top of the big bed he forgot that the uncertainty or anxiety had ever existed at all. He needed her very urgently and he could not wait this time, could not wait and do things nice and slow the way she usually liked to do things. He was in a hurry.

"Honey, you'll rip my dress!"

"I'll buy you a new one."

The voice did not even sound like his own. And the hands that hurried with her clothing were much stronger, much more certain of themselves than his hands. The hands, the clever and hungry hands that touched that perfect body all over, they were not his hands at all.

He took her and it was good, very good. It was hard and tough and fast and the blood pounded against his brain. It was an affirmation, a declaration, and when it was over he felt not exhausted but reinvigorated, as if he had taken a vitamin pill instead of a woman.

Usually, after they had made love, he would lie limp and weak in the shelter of her arms. This time, however, he rolled away from her as soon as the initial glow had passed from him. He lay on his side, not facing her, and for some reason he did not want to look at her just then.

A moment later he was on his feet, drawing the covers over her nude body and heading for the bathroom. "I want to take a shower," he called over his shoulder. "Then I'll go see about the papers. You stay right here until I come back."

He turned on the shower and stepped into the tub. From the bed Honour Mercy could hear the water pounding down in steady torrent. Then, above the roar of the shower, she heard another sound, one she had never heard before.

He was singing.

After the abortive phone call to Canelli, Joshua Crawford had sat at his desk for perhaps twenty-five seconds. Then, all at once, he sprang to his feet and hurried out of the office without saying goodbye to anybody. He hailed a cab and left it at the corner of Third Avenue and 24th Street in front of an establishment known only as HOCK SHOP. That was what the black letters on the dingy yellow clapboard proclaimed and that was what the three golden balls were there to signify. That was enough.

The owner, a round-shouldered man with thick glasses who looked like all pawnbrokers everywhere, was speedily persuaded to sell a .38-caliber police positive revolver to one John Brown for the sum of two hundred dollars. The pawnbroker, who had bought the gun from a sneak thief for ten dollars, was pleased with the transaction. Joshua Crawford, who didn't give much of a damn what the gun cost him, was equally pleased. He put the gun in his briefcase, tucked the case under his arm, and strode out of the store.

He called Selma from a pay station in a candy store two doors down the street. "I'm working late," he told her, hardly caring whether or not she believed him. "I'll see you tomorrow."

Another cab took him to Grand Central. He bought a ticket on the Empire State, boarded the train and collapsed into a coach seat. The train seemed to crawl and the briefcase on his lap weighed a ton but he lived through the trip without knowing just how he managed it. It was a few minutes to nine when he was on his way out of the Albany terminal with the briefcase once again under his arm.

Finding them, he knew, was going to be a problem. He had to nose them out all on his own, and he had to do it without attracting any undue attention, and this was not going to be the easiest thing in the world. Then, when he did find them, he had to get to Richie without Honour Mercy seeing him. Then, and only then, he had to put a bullet into Richie, a bullet that would forever eliminate Richie as any sort of competition whatsoever.

Then he had to get away. If nobody saw him and if he got clear of the scene of the crime, then he ought to be safe all the way. There was no connection between him and Richie other than Honour Mercy, and it was extremely unlikely that she would have any suspicion at all that he had killed Richie. The gun was untraceable. The anonymity of a coach seat on the Empire was complete.

But the big thing went beyond guns and witnesses. It was simply that the police would never suspect him, and unless they started investigating him, they would have to leave the crime forever unsolved. If they had any idea it was him, they would get him in no time, no matter how much trouble he took in covering his trail. That was why murderers got caught—because they had motives for their murders. If a man had no motive, or if his motive was sufficiently obscure, getting away with murder was a lot easier than it sounded.

But first he had to find them. And before that he had to eat—there was no point in killing a man on an empty stomach. He went to Keeler's, on State Street, because it was supposed to be the best restaurant in Albany. The steak they brought him was tender and juicy and the baked potato was powdery with a crisp skin. The coffee fit the three traditional tests—it was black as hell, strong as death, and sweet as love. He had three cups of it and felt one hell of a lot better when the caffeine got to work on his system.

It was almost ten when he left the restaurant. The night was cold and clear, the streets virtually empty. He started walking downtown on State Street, wondering just how he was going to find that idiot Parsons, when, impossibly, he saw him.

At first he did not believe it. For one thing, the guy a block ahead of him wasn't walking like Richie had walked. His head was held high and his shoulders were back; there was even a certain amount of spring to his step. That didn't jibe with the picture Crawford had of him.

But it *was* Richie. Crawford got a look at his face when he stopped to study a window display at a sporting goods store, and there was no longer any question in his mind. It was Richie, and Richie was just standing there waiting to be killed, and now all he had to do was catch up with him and take the revolver from the briefcase and blow a hole in Richie Parsons' head.

Which would be a pleasure.

But how?

He kept following Richie, staying about a block behind him, hoping he would leave the main street and find himself a nice quiet alley to get shot in. That would be the best way, the easiest way all around. Shooting him dead on State Street would be a pretty tricky proposition, especially since the damned gun didn't have a silencer. He had tried to buy a silencer, but that ass of a pawnbroker hadn't had one to sell him. When the gun went off, it was going to sound like a cannon, and State Street was hardly the place to shoot off a cannon.

When Richie went into the Conning Towers Hotel, Crawford felt like crying. But there wasn't a hell of a lot he could do about it. He had missed his chance for the night, but there was always a chance that he would get a crack at Richie in the morning, or later on if the two of them didn't go back to New York the next day. The identification Richie had come for might take a while to prepare, in which case Richie Parsons would never leave Albany alive. If Crawford never got another chance at him, then Canelli could have the job in the city and Crawford would do the fingering. That would be safer in the long run, anyhow, even though there was a certain personal satisfaction in doing the job on his own.

Joshua Crawford decided to have a cup of coffee in the beanery across the street from the Conning Towers. The coffee was not at all good and he almost left after the first sip. But for some reason he stayed, sipping at it from time to time and smoking constantly, his eyes flashing from the glowing end of his cigarette to the impressive entrance of the Conning Towers.

If he had not lingered over the coffee, he would not have been there to see Richie Parsons emerge alone from the hotel about a half-hour after entering it. When he did, a jolt of excitement went through him and he dropped a dime on the counter and left the diner in a hurry. He waited until Richie was half a block ahead and then began to follow him.

This time Richie didn't stay on State Street. This time he walked into just the sort of neighborhood Crawford would have selected—a warehouse district, empty of people and homes and apartment buildings. An ideal setting for a quick and quiet murder.

Crawford began walking faster. Without breaking stride he opened the briefcase, got the gun in his right hand and closed the briefcase again. He kept walking faster and in no time at all he was just a few feet behind Richie.

The gun was already pointed at Richie when he turned around. He stared and his eyes took in first Crawford and then the gun, and then both Crawford and the gun at once. For the shadow of an instant he stared and his face was a study.

Then there was a hole in it.

## Chapter 8

There was a full-length mirror on the back of the bathroom door and Honour Mercy, emerging from her shower, toweled the steam from the surface of the mirror and looked at herself, trying to find comfort in the appearance of her body.

But there was no comfort there, there or anywhere else. "He's going to leave me," she told the girl in the mirror. "He doesn't need me anymore, and he's going to leave me."

She wondered if Richie himself knew yet that he would be leaving her soon, and she thought that he was probably beginning to suspect it. The difference in his attitude, the way he had sung in the shower, the fact that he was now out of the hotel somewhere; they all gave indication of the change in Richie Parsons that was making her unnecessary to him.

A month ago, Richie wouldn't have dared set foot it Albany. Once in Albany, he wouldn't have dreamed of registering at the city's most expensive hotel. Having rented a hotel room, no power on earth would have moved him from that hotel room, to roam the streets of his home town late at night.

She understood some of the causes of the change. She was a major cause. When he had been at his most bewildered, his most frightened, she had given him refuge and friendship. More than that, she had given him an appreciative sexual partner, without which he would never have emerged from his cringing, cowering shell. She had built up his ego, supported him, comforted him, protected him, and his personality had developed character.

There were other factors, too. The longer he had successfully avoided capture by the authorities, the less the authorities were a menace in his mind. And with that threat waning, he gradually had less reason to cower, less reason to be afraid.

The decision to come to Albany was the final step in the change. He had made no decisions at all since he had run away from the Air Force; Honour Mercy had made all the decisions for both of them. Now, at last, he had made a decision of his own. And his decision had been to brave his terror where it would be the fiercest. In his own home town.

As she thought about it, it occurred to her that there was a step missing in the chain. Richie was a different person today—had been a different person when she met him at Grand Central—from the Richie of yesterday. Something had happened that had forced him to make the decision; and then he had made the decision, and the change had been complete. But what had forced the decision?

The man who had asked him for his draft card? She considered that, and rejected it. No, it would have had to be more than that. An incident like that would simply have sent Richie running for shelter to their apartment, and he wouldn't have ventured out on the street again for days. There had been something else; something more than what he had told her.

For the first time, Richie had kept something from her, had

lied to her. And that knowledge only confirmed the idea that Richie was going to leave her.

She dried herself hurriedly, taking no enjoyment from it. Usually, she luxuriated in the shower, and in the drying after that, with a huge soft towel like this, rubbing her skin until it tingled and shone. Tonight, she couldn't think about such things. She patted herself dry as quickly as possible and went out to the other room to look at the clock-radio on the nightstand.

Richie had said he was going to be out for an hour at the most. He had gone out for a walk a little before ten—proving to himself his new independence and fearlessness—and then he had gone out at eleven o'clock exactly. This time, to talk to the man he knew who might be able to arrange false identification for him. And he had promised he would be back within the hour; he would be back by midnight for sure.

The clock-radio said that it was now quarter to one.

"He isn't coming back," she said. She said it aloud, without realizing she was going to, and then she listened to the echo of the words, and wondered if she'd been right.

Would he do it this way? He couldn't, that would be too cruel, too unfair. To leave her stranded here, in a city she didn't know, in this expensive hotel room, with no money, with nothing—that would be too terribly cruel.

But it would be the easiest way out for him, and Honour Mercy knew her Richie well. Richie would always take the easiest way out.

If he isn't home by one o'clock, she told herself, I'll know he's left me.

Fifteen minutes later, she said to herself: If he isn't home by one-thirty, I'll know for sure that he's left me.

When the big hand was on the six and the little hand was on the one, she started to cry.

When the big hand was on the eight and the little hand had edged over toward the two, she finished crying.

By the time the big hand had reached the nine and the little hand hadn't done much of anything, she was dressed and lip-sticked, and ready to go.

Honour Mercy Bane was a pragmatist. "Go to Newport and be a bad woman," her parents told her, and she went. "We've got to pack up and get out of Newport," Richie said, and she packed. "Talk to me," said Joshua Crawford, and she talked.

And now, now she was alone and penniless in a strange city, with a huge hotel bill that would be hers alone to pay, and once again she was a pragmatist. It was quarter to two in the morning, and time for Honour Mercy to go to work.

Honour Mercy had learned a lot, changed a lot, grown a lot since Newport, too. Six months ago, in this situation, she would have been at a loss. She would have tried to hustle on one of the wrong streets and spent the night in jail. Now, she knew better. She left the room, pressed the button for the elevator, and said to the operator on the way down, "Where can a girl find some work in this town, do you know?" Because elevator operators in hotels always did know.

He looked at her blankly, either not yet understanding or playing dumb for reasons of his own. "Lots of Civil Service jobs with the state around here," he said.

"That isn't exactly what I was thinking."

He studied her, and chewed his cud, and finally made up his mind. "Management don't allow hustling in the hotel," he said.

"Don't tell me where I can't," she told him. "Tell me where I can."

"I get off duty here at six o'clock," he said.

She understood at once, and forced a smile for his benefit. "I imagine I'll be back by then."

He nodded. "When you go outside," he said, "walk down the hill to Green Street. Turn right."

She waited for more directions, but there were no more forthcoming, so she said, "Thanks."

"Don't mention it," he said.

The elevator reached the main floor, and she walked through the empty lobby to the street, and started down the State Street hill.

Six blocks south and one block west of the Conning Towers, Joshua Crawford sat in a chair beside the CID man's desk and said, "I just don't remember a thing. It's all a blank."

"Lawyer Crawford," said the CID man, with heavy emphasis on the first word, "I hope you aren't going to try for a temporary insanity plea. You had the gun on you. We can prove premeditation with no trouble at all."

Crawford rubbed a damp palm across his face. "I *must* have been crazy," he whispered, meaning it sincerely. "I *must* have been crazy." He looked pleadingly at the CID man. "My wife," he said. "This is going to be hell for my wife."

The CID man waited.

"In many ways," said Crawford seriously, "my wife is an excellent woman." His hand came up to his face again.

The CID man waited. He was bored. He had nothing to do but wait now. They always cried before confessing.

The first two blocks of Green Street were dark and narrow and lifeless, except for an occasional derelict asleep beside an empty bottle in a doorway. The third block was just as narrow, but brightly lit from a double row of bars, and people were constantly on the move. Cars were parked on both sides of the street, leaving only one narrow lane open in the middle for the one-way traffic, of which there was practically none. The derelicts who were still shakily on their feet were all over this block, mingling with short, slender, bright-eyed homosexuals, hard-looking hustlers, strange-uniformed sailors—since Albany is also a port city, shipping grain and manufactured goods to the European markets—and clusters of skinny, black-jacketed teenagers. It didn't look good to Honour Mercy; it was lower and harder and more primitive than anything she'd ever run into before, and so she kept on walking.

The fourth block was half-bright and half-dark. Bars were scattered here and there on both sides of the street, but crammed in with them were dark, empty-windowed tenements. And in the doorways and ground-floor windows of the tenements were women, watching the street. This was closer to the world Honour

Mercy knew, and so she stopped at the first dark doorway on her side of the street and looked at the Negro woman standing there. "I just got to town," she said.

"Come in here off the street!" hissed the woman.

Honour Mercy, surprised, did as she was told, and the woman said, "What you want?"

"I just got here," repeated Honour Mercy. "I don't know what things are like."

"They ain't good," said the woman. "The goddamn police is on the rampage." She laughed harshly at Honour Mercy's blank look. "No, they ain't honest," she said. "They just greedy. They want all the bread they can get. The only way to make a dime in this town is hustle on your own and take your chances on being picked up." She looked out at the street and ducked back, clutching Honour Mercy's arm. "Get back in here!"

Honour Mercy, not understanding what was going on, cowered with the woman in the darkest corner of the entranceway. Outside, a three-year-old Buick drove slowly by, two men in the front seat. The car was painted black, with small gray letters on the front door reading, "POLICE," and a red light, now off, attached to the top of the right fender.

The car slid by, slow and silent, and the hand gripping Honour Mercy's arm slowly relaxed. Honour Mercy, impressed by it all, whispered, "Who was that?"

"The King," said the woman, and the way she said it, it wasn't as funny as it should have been. "He runs this section. He's the only cop in the city dares walk down this street alone. He goes into a bar—crowded, jumpin'—and he picks out the man he's after, and he says, 'You come with me.' And he walks out, with the guy at his heels, and nobody stops him. Any other cop in this town try that, he'd get his badge shoved down his throat."

"How can *he* do it?"

The woman shrugged. "He breaks heads," she said. "And he's straight. He don't take a penny, and he don't make a phony rap. Get rid of him, you get somebody bad down here to take his place."

When Honour Mercy left the hotel, it had seemed simple enough. She would go to work. Now, it didn't seem so simple any more. This city had a set-up unlike anything she'd ever seen before.

"You got a pad?" the woman asked suddenly.

Honour Mercy shook her head.

"No good," said the woman. "You stuck to guys with cars. That means you got to stay on the sidewalk, where they can see you. And where the law can see you. You ought to wait till you get a pad."

"I need money tonight," said Honour Mercy. It wasn't strictly true. The hotel wouldn't start asking for money for a day or two at least. What Honour Mercy needed tonight was to work, to be doing something that would take her mind off the defection of Richie Parsons.

The woman shrugged again. "Then you got to hit the pavement. Look out for one-tone cars, specially Buicks and Oldsmobiles. That's the law, whether it says so on the car or not."

"Thanks a lot," said Honour Mercy. "I appreciate it."

"We all in the same racket," said the woman.

"What—what are the prices around here?"

The woman looked her over. "You're white," she said. "And you're young. You could get away with charging ten."

Ten. That was low pay indeed, low, low pay after New York. Honour Mercy decided right there to get enough money together to get back to New York as quickly as possible. Back to New York, where the organization was so much smoother, the prices so much higher, the clientele so much better. Back to New York, and, come to think of it, back to Joshua Crawford.

Joshua was going to ask her to be his mistress. She knew that, but she'd avoided acknowledging it before this, because it would have brought up the problem of Richie. But now that Richie had left her, there was no problem. She would get the money quickly, get back to New York, and she would become Joshua Crawford's mistress. It would be a good life.

"Thanks again," she said to the woman, and left the darkness of the doorway.

She walked for twenty minutes before she got a customer. Single-color Buicks and Oldsmobiles had driven by, slowly, the drivers watching the sidewalks, but she hadn't even glanced at them as they passed her. She had walked purposefully, as though to a set destination, when cars like that passed her, and she hadn't been stopped.

The customer—or customers—arrived in a late-forties Ford, amateurishly painted gold and black. There were four teenagers in the car, and the driver slowed to a crawl, matching Honour Mercy's speed, and they went half a block that way before he murmured. "Hey. You lookin' for somebody?"

She turned and gave him the big smile. "Nobody in particular," she said.

He stopped the car completely. "Come on over here."

She went, studying the driver's face. He was about seventeen, sharp-nosed and dissatisfied-looking, with a crewcut. The other three were all in the shadows within the car, but she knew they would look very much like the driver.

When she got to the car, the driver said, "How much?"

"I charge ten dollars—" she noticed the change of expression in time "—but with a group like this, of course, it's cheaper."

"How much?" he repeated, more warily.

She thought rapidly. Seventeen-year-old boys, she knew from past experience, had a habit of not lasting very long. She could probably go through all four of them in fifteen minutes, including time lost changing partners. If they didn't have to drive very far to find a place where they could park in privacy, and if they didn't waste too much getting down to business once they'd parked, she might even be able to get back in time for one more trick tonight. Thinking of this, and judging, as best she could, the amount of money the boy and his friends would be able and willing to spend, she came, almost without a pause in the conversation, to a number.

"Twenty-five dollars."

She waited through the whispered consultation. Once they'd figured out that that was only six dollars and twenty-five cents apiece, the consultation was rapidly over. The door to the rear seat opened, a tall blond-haired boy stepped out, and the driver said, "Okay. Climb aboard."

To her left was the blond boy. To her right was a short, black-haired, large-nosed boy, who looked terribly nervous. Up front, the boy beside the driver was black-haired and spectacled. She gave each of them a mental tag, to keep them straight. There was the Blond, the Driver, the Glasses, and the Nervous.

The car turned left at the next intersection and drove through dark and twisting streets. The Blond put his hand on her knee and squeezed experimentally. Remembering that she wanted them to be in condition to make short work of it, she smiled at him and squeezed back. He grinned and slid his hand up her leg, under the skirt, then murmured, "Why don't you get the panties off right now? Save some time."

"All right."

It took a lot of squirming, in the crowded back seat, to get them off, and she made sure she did a lot of the squirming against Nervous, to her right. She wanted to get him in the mood, too, and she was afraid that would take some doing.

The squirming did the trick. When she was settled again, the Blond's hand was once more up under her skirt, and the Nervous had a hand inside her blouse. He tugged at the bra and whispered, betraying the fact that he was still nervous, "Take that off, too."

More squirming this time, complicated by the fact that the Blond's hand was doing distracting things beneath the skirt, and finally her blouse was open and her bra off and lying on the ledge behind the seat. The Nervous bent forward and kissed her breast, and the Blond's hand was still moving beneath her skirt. She closed her eyes and stopped thinking.

The car was on a main street for a while, and then off that, and there were occasional glimpses of the river off to the left. They passed warehouses and trucking concerns and bakeries, all closed and dark and silent now. They passed the spot where

Richie Parsons had stopped living three hours before, but there was no longer any sign that there had been violence here tonight. This was also the spot where the cruising prowl car had so unexpectedly caught Joshua Crawford, open-faced and panting, the gun still in his hand, in the hard bright beams of its headlights, but the spot bore no witness of him, either. The car drove by, and farther on it turned left again, toward the river, and then right, and stopped.

Honour Mercy was ready. She wouldn't have to fake her responses with these boys. But she still retained enough presence of mind to say, "Money in advance, boys. That's standard."

The four of them got out of the car, leaving Honour Mercy in the back seat, and consulted together outside. The Driver came back, finally, with the money. A five-dollar bill, a bunch of wrinkled singles, and two dollars in change. Honour Mercy stashed it all in her purse, stashed the purse on the window ledge with her bra, and smiled at the Driver. "Are you first?"

"You bet I am," he said.

She'd given him the right nickname. He came at her fast and brutal, crushing her down in the cramped back seat, driving her down and back, half-smothering her. But his very force betrayed him. He was finished before he was barely started, leaving Honour Mercy moving alone. But he seemed satisfied as he crawled out of the car again, and walked over to the waiting group.

The Blond was second, and he had read books on the subject. He tried to come at her slow and gradually, full of technique. Under normal circumstances, she would have followed his lead, because she enjoyed the niceties of technique, no matter how academic. But there had been the hands and lips all over her on the ride, and the Driver had just finished with her, and she was in no mood to be gradual. She sunk her teeth into his shoulder and her nails into his buttocks and he forgot the textbooks.

They stopped together, rigid and straining and open-mouthed, and when he left, the inside of the car was beginning to be heavy with the acrid perfume of love.

Glasses came next, and he had a variety of ideas. There were other things he wanted done first, some of them very difficult in the back seat of a late-forties Ford, and she had a chance to cool down a bit and to begin to think again.

Glasses had her spend too much time with the preliminaries, and all at once the main event was canceled. But he smiled and shrugged and said, "That's the way it goes." And she knew that that was the way he had wanted it all along, and she wondered if he understood yet that he was homosexual.

Nervous came last, and Nervous wasn't even ready. She realized, with a sinking feeling, that this was Nervous's first time. The backseat was cramped, the air in the car was now too heavy for comfort, and she knew that she was a sweat-stained, disheveled and panting mess, stimulating to a man, perhaps, but not to a boy coming to sex for the first time.

She did what she could for him, smiling at him, talking gently with him, telling him that lots of men needed help in getting ready. She gave him the help he needed, half-afraid that it just wasn't going to work out, and slowly she felt the interest growing within him. And when he was ready, she didn't try to rush it, she tried to make it last, because she understood how important it was to him, this first time.

But nothing could have made him last. He was here and gone

again in two shakes of his nervous tail, and then it was all over and she was alone in the back seat of the car and slipping back into her clothes.

They waited outside until she was ready. When she was dressed, she climbed out of the car, needing fresh air and a bit of walking to revive her completely.

The four of them were clustered around the front of the car, and she glanced at them, and all of a sudden she realized what was going to happen. She panicked, standing frozen beside the car, not knowing what to do.

The money, that was the important thing. The purse was still on the window ledge, and she tried to be casual in her movements as she opened the rear door again and got the purse.

But when she got back out of the car, they were bunched around her, and the Driver was standing directly in front of her, grinning bitterly and saying, "Where you going, Sweetheart?"

"Please," she said. "I need the money. I need it."

"Don't we all," he said.

Nervous, a step back of the rest, piped up, "Let her have the money, Danny. We can afford it."

The Driver—Danny—whirled and snapped, "Shut up, you clown. Now she knows my name."

"Let her keep the money," Nervous insisted, but it was weak insistence, and Honour Mercy knew he was a poor, albeit willing, ally.

If she was going to get out of this, she'd have to get out by herself. While they were all distracted by Nervous, she might just be able to—

She got two steps, and the Driver had her by the arm and was spinning her around, shoving her back against the side of the car. "Where do you think you're going, Sweetheart?" he asked again, and hit her solidly in the stomach.

The punch knocked the wind out of her, and she sagged against the car, clutching her stomach, her mouth open as she gasped for air. And the shrill voice of Nervous was sounding again, but she knew it was no use, and the sound stopped when the Driver snarled, "Shut that idiot up."

She could do no more than stand, weakly, leaning against the car, trying for breath. When the purse was ripped out of her hands, she could do nothing to stop it. And when she heard the Driver say, "I think I'm going to teach this little bitch a lesson," she could do nothing to protect herself or to get away.

One of the others—Glasses?—said, "What the hell, Danny, leave her alone. We got the money."

"She wants a lesson," insisted Danny. And he back-handed her across the side of the face.

She would have fallen, but he caught her and shoved her back against the side of the car again, and held her with one hand cruelly gripping her breast while he slapped her, openhanded, back and forth across the face. She cried out, finally having breath, and he switched at once, punching her twice, hard, in the stomach. As she doubled, he punched her twice more, on the point of each breast.

She screamed with the searing pain of it and fell to her knees. He slapped her—forehand, backhand, forehand, backhand—and dragged her to her feet once more, shoving her back against the car, and as he did so he kneed her, and ground the knuckles of his right hand into her side, just under the ribcage.

He wouldn't let her fall. He held her with a clutching, twisting hand on her breast, and his other hand beat at her, face and breast and stomach and side, open-hand and closed fist.

The Blond and Glasses pulled him away from her finally, and she collapsed onto the dank, weed-choked ground, unable to move or make a sound, capable only of breathing and feeling the pain stabbing through her body from every place that he had hit.

After a moment, she heard the car start, and she was terrified that now he was going to drive over her, but the sound of the motor receded to silence, and she knew they had gone away.

She lay for half an hour unmoving, until the worst pain subsided, and then she struggled to a sitting position, and had to stop again, because movement brought the pain back, hard and tight, and she was afraid she would faint. And then she hoped she would faint.

But she didn't faint, and after another while she managed to get to her feet. Behind her was the street that would lead her back to the downtown section. Ahead of her was the faint rustle of the river. To either side of her were the dark hulks of commercial buildings.

She knew she must look horrible, and with the lessening of the pain she could think about that. If she showed herself on the street looking like this, the police would pick her up right away. And even if she managed to avoid the police, she would never get through the hotel lobby.

Moving painfully, she made her way toward the sound of the river. There was a narrow, steep incline between two buildings which overhung the river's edge, and old wooden pilings to lean against on the way down. The water was brackish and foul-smelling, filled with sewage and industrial waste, the filthy pollution of a river beside which industrial cities had been built. But it was water.

She knelt gingerly, and pushed her hands into the water. It was cold, and she waited, unmoving, letting the chill move up her arms to her torso, reviving her, restoring her, and then she lay prone and splashed the fouled water over her face, washing away the smudges and stains of her beating.

She almost went to sleep, and her head would have fallen forward and her face would have been underwater. She caught herself in time, and backed hastily away from the edge, terrified at the nearness of death.

She used her panties to towel her face and hands and arms, then threw the sodden garment into the water, and turned toward the street.

Midway, she found her purse, lying on the ground. She carried it out to the street, where a streetlight across the way gave her enough light to check its contents.

There was no money in it, but nothing else had been touched. Her hand mirror was there, and she inspected her face critically, seeing that the signs of the beating were still there. And her hair was a mass of tangled knots, damp and filthy.

She had a comb and lipstick and powder. She repaired the damage as best she could, and when she was finished, she looked presentable enough, if she didn't get too close to anybody. She smoothed and adjusted her clothing, rubbing out some of the stains, and started off for the hotel.

She was still weak. Every once in a while, she had to stop and lean against a building for a moment, to catch her breath and wait for the dizziness to go away. And when she came to the bottom of the State Street hill, she looked up at the hotel, so high above her, and she thought she would never be able to get up that long steep hill.

But she made it, finally, and entered the hotel lobby softly, circling away from the desk, where the night-clerk was busy with file cards, and getting to the elevator without being stopped.

The operator looked at her with surprise. "What happened to you?"

She, shook her head. "Nothing. Never mind."

"Listen," he said. "There's cops in your room."

She stared at him.

The weakness was coming in again, and she thought that this time she would faint for sure, but the operator was still talking, and what he said next drove the weakness away and left her pale and trembling, but only too conscious.

"Yep," he said, nodding, chewing his cud, happy to be the news-bearer. "Some crazy queer shot him. Right between the eyes. Signed a confession and everything, and then jumped right out a window." He shook his head, grinning. "Them coppers are sure mad," he said. "It don't look good when a prisoner manages to kill himself that way. Hey! Where you going?"

But she didn't answer him, because she didn't know.

She didn't know until she was at the foot of State Street once more, and looking at the signs on a telephone pole. The top sign was shield-shaped, and said, "U.S. Route 9." The bottom sign was rectangular and said, "NEW YORK," with an arrow underneath.

New York. She nodded, and noticed she'd dropped the purse somewhere. She was empty-handed. Not that it mattered.

New York. She would be Joshua's mistress.

She started walking in the direction the arrow indicated. A chill breeze snaked up under her skirt, and she was no longer wearing panties, but she didn't notice. She just walked, and when false dawn was streaking the sky to her left, Albany was behind her.

# CHAPTER 9

Tires screeched and kicked gravel as the big car pulled off the road and squealed to a stop on the shoulder. The driver leaned across the seat, opened the door and stuck his head out.

"Want a lift?"

She ran to the car. In the back of her mind she heard her mother cautioning her not to accept rides with strange men. But then there had been many things that her mother had told her. It was no time to start listening to those things.

"Where you headed?"

"New York."

"Hop in."

She hopped in. The car was a new Buick and it was big. So was the driver. A shock of straw-colored hair topped his big boulder of a head. His hands were huge and they held the steering wheel as if it might fall apart unless he personally held it together. When she had closed the door, he let out the clutch and put the accelerator pedal on the floor. The car responded as though it was scared of him.

"Nice car you got."

The man nodded, agreeing. "She'll do a hundred easy," he told her. "One-twenty if I push her a little. The mileage isn't much, but if I wanted to worry about mileage I'd get myself a bicycle. I want a car that'll move when I want her to move."

He had what he wanted, in that case. When Honour Mercy looked at the speedometer she noticed that the little red needle was pointing at sixty-five and edging over toward seventy.

"That's why I travel this road," he went on. "Thruway takes you from Albany down to New York just the same, but those troopers watch the Thruway pretty close. Limit's sixty and when you go much over sixty-five they stop you and hit you with a ticket. That's no fun. Costs a guy twenty, thirty bucks for the ticket plus a few bucks in tolls. No fun at all."

The needle was pointing at seventy-five.

"You come from Albany?"

She nodded.

"Figure on hitching? Reason I ask is I didn't see you standing with your thumb out. Just walking. Looked like you were trying to walk clear to New York."

This was precisely what she had been doing, but she didn't think the man would accept it as a logical explanation. "I was having trouble getting a ride," she said. "So I just started walking for a few minutes. I thought maybe I'd have more luck if I went on down to the first intersection."

He nodded and she decided that she had picked the right reply. "I'm not from Albany myself," the man was saying. "Pass through there a lot, though. I live up in Rome; got a business up there. You know where that is?"

She didn't.

"Yes," she said.

"Have to run down to New York a lot," he went on. "On

business. So I come through Albany. Don't stop there too often, but this time I made a breakfast stop on the outskirts. I like a cup of coffee now and then when I drive. Keeps my mind on what I'm doing."

The needle pointed at eighty.

"Quite a thing up there last night, wasn't there? I had a look at the paper while I was eating; just had time to skim over the front page. Quite a thing. Double killing and all. You hear about it?"

She shook her head. Richie had evidently made the papers, she thought. Maybe if she just let this man run off at the mouth about it she could learn a little more about what had happened.

"Quite a thing," he said. "Quite a thing. Young kid checked into a hotel with a girl, went out for a walk and a guy came up behind him and blew his head off. Shot him smack dab in the face and there wasn't a hell of a lot of his face left afterwards. Least that's what the paper said. They seem to build these things up."

She shuddered. He looked at her and misinterpreted the shudder as normal female revulsion and patted her knee to soothe her. When he touched her she wondered how long it would take him to make a pass at her. She knew he was going to; knew that was why he had picked her up in the first place. He would make a pass at her and she would let him do whatever he wanted to do with her. He was going to New York and he would take her there, and in exchange he had a right to the temporary use of her body. That was fundamental.

"Who did it?" she managed. "Did they catch the man who did it?"

"Sure did," the big man said. His hand was still on her knee, not to calm her, not now, and the speedometer needle was moving toward ninety. She hoped they would live to get back to New York. Because that was all that mattered—getting to New York and becoming Joshua's mistress. That was what she had to do and the man with his big hand on her knee was just another means to the end.

"Caught him in the act," the man said. "Just about in the act. Red-handed, the way they say it. Paper said he was standing there with the smoking gun still in his hand when the police took hold of him. Didn't make a fuss or anything."

He lapsed into temporary silence, becoming preoccupied with her knee, and she had to prompt him. "You said double killing. Who else did he kill?"

"Didn't kill nobody else. Killed himself. Police had him up at the station house and he took a dive through the window. Fell a couple stories and that was the end of him."

She shuddered again, as memory tried to intrude, then regretted it because it only got the hand more interested in her knee. Now who in the world would want to kill Richie? It didn't make the slightest bit of sense to her, and she decided that it must have been a case of mistaken identity.

"Do they know why the man did it?"

"Nope," the driver said. "Don't know a thing. All they know is his name and the name of the guy he killed. The young fellow's name was Shaw, Anthony or Andy or something of the sort."

For the merest shadow of a second her heart jumped at the thought that Richie hadn't been killed after all, that the dead boy was somebody else. Then she remembered that Shaw was the name Richie had picked out for himself. That was the way he'd signed the register at the hotel.

"Can't remember the other one's name," the driver continued. "It's on the tip of my tongue but I'll be damned if I remember it. Just took a quick look through the paper before it was time to hit the road again."

The "quick look" had nearly committed the whole story to his memory. Honour Mercy could picture him, gulping down his coffee and reading the grisly article with his eyes bugging out of his head.

"Seems I ought to be able to remember the name," the driver said. "But I can't."

"Was he a . . . gangster?"

The man shook his head. "Nope," he said. "Wasn't even from Albany. Came from New York. One of them New York lawyers. I've met some of those fellows and I wouldn't put anything past them. Sharp ones, them."

A warning bell sounded inside the back of Honour Mercy's head. It wasn't possible, she told herself. It was a coincidence, that was all. It couldn't be, just plain couldn't be.

But she was afraid. Memory was crouched, ready to spring. She looked out the window at the ground that was passing by very swiftly, then looked at the speedometer needle that told how fast the ground was passing by, and then looked at the hand on her knee.

Not Joshua. She was going to Joshua, that was the important thing. It hadn't been him.

"His name," she said, slowly. "Funny thing you can't remember it."

"Hardly makes a difference."

"I mean," she said, "the way you remembered the other one,

the boy who got shot. Just seems funny that you couldn't remember the name of the one who shot him."

"Yes, funny," the man said. "Right on the tip of my tongue, too. Paper must of mentioned it a dozen times, if they mentioned it once. And I'm usually pretty good when it comes to remembering."

*Think,* she thought. Say it wasn't Joshua.

"Damned if it isn't coming back to me now," the man said, excited at the prospect of demonstrating just how good he was at remembering things. "Some sort of a Bible name, now that I think about it."

She couldn't breathe.

"Sure," the man said. A vein was throbbing on his broad forehead. "Sure, that's what it was. It's coming now. Who was it fought that battle at Jericho? The one they got that song about?"

"Joshua," she whispered.

"Yep," the man said, happy now. "Joshua. Last name was something like 'Crawfish,' but that ain't it. It'll probably come to me in another minute if I think about it awhile."

She wanted to tell him not to waste his time but she couldn't because she knew that if she opened her mouth she would scream.

She was in her apartment off Central Park West, alone, and she ached all over. Her body ached, first from the four boys, and then from the big man who had driven her to New York, and whom she had obligingly permitted to lead her into the privacy of a motel room en route.

And her lower lip ached from biting it, and her head ached

because her brain was spinning around. But the worst ache of all was somewhere inside.

She was alone.

That was it. She was alone, completely alone, and she had not been alone since that time when she stood with a ratty cardboard suitcase in her hand in Newport's Greyhound station.

Alone.

There was no one with her, because Richie was dead, and there was no one to call, because Joshua was dead. And, because Richie and Joshua had been the only two people in her world, this left her, according to the inexorable laws of mathematics, alone.

Alone.

And, incidentally, penniless.

That was silly, because she had quite a bit of money in the bank. But it was after three and the bank was closed, so for the moment the money in the bank was quite useless. Actually she could do without money until the bank opened for business again in the morning; the refrigerator was filled with food and all she had to do was cook it and eat it. And even if the refrigerator had been empty, she could easily last until morning without eating. The big man had bought her a meal which she had forced herself to eat. She wouldn't starve.

But if she stayed in the apartment she might go out of her mind. That's what would happen—she would go crazy. She would look at the walls and look at the ceiling until the walls closed in and the ceiling fell on her, and she would go crazy.

Because she was so damned alone.

For a long time there had been no problem. She was with

Richie and the two of them shared an apartment and a bed and a way of life. There was a pattern and she lived within the pattern.

Then there wasn't Richie, all of a sudden, but there was still a pattern. The pattern centered around Joshua. She would go back to New York and let Joshua ask her to be his mistress, and then she would live with him, sharing his apartment and his bed.

Another pattern.

And then, out of the blue, there wasn't Joshua any more. And there wasn't any pattern. There was simply Honour Mercy Bane alone by herself, all alone, terribly alone, with nothing to do and no place to go. In a day, two patterns had been shattered, in twenty-four hours or so, Richie had gone and Joshua had gone, and they had both left her alone.

And now?

Now there was no pattern. Nothing fit together. There were any number of things she could do, but nothing added up to a pattern, nothing gave her a life that got rid of the aloneness.

She would stay in the apartment, have something to eat and go to sleep. In the morning they would call her and tell her what tricks were lined up for her, and she would go out and handle her tricks and take home her money. She would live alone in her apartment and save her money and turn her tricks, and that would be her life.

And the walls would close in and the ceiling would fall, and one day would follow the other without shape or pattern, and she would go mad.

She would stay in the apartment, have something to eat and go to sleep. In the morning she would go to the bank and draw out all her money and buy a ticket to Newport. When she got to

Newport she would find Madge and get her old job back, or get Madge to line her up a job at one of the other houses.

And she would live by herself in an empty room at the Casterbridge Hotel, and she would eat Gil Gluck's tasteless food and walk up and down a flight of stairs for eight hours every day, and one day would follow the other without shape or pattern, and she would go mad.

She would stay in the apartment, have something to eat and go to sleep. In the morning she would go to the bank and draw out all her money and buy a ticket to Coldwater. When she got to Coldwater she would find her parents and fall on her knees and beg forgiveness, and Prudence and Abraham Bane would forgive her and take her back and she would get a job and live at home with her parents.

And she would eat grits and ribs and fatback, and she would read the Bible every day and go to sleep by ten, and people would stare after her when she passed them on the street, and one day would follow the other without shape or pattern, and she would go mad.

Alone.

And empty.

She got up from the bed, and that helped a little. She had a bite to eat, a pair of scrambled eggs with some cheddar cheese melted in them, and that helped. She took a bath and washed away the odor of the man who had driven her from Albany to New York, and that helped.

She left the apartment. That also helped. She walked halfway to the subway stop before she remembered that she had no money and consequently couldn't buy a token for the train. She thought that she could stop someone on the street and ask for a token, or go to the man at the turnstile and talk him into letting her crawl under free. But she decided instead that she might as well walk, that where she was going was only a little over a mile and that the walk would do her good.

She headed downtown.


Eighth Avenue, which is what Central Park West turns into when Central Park is no longer to the east of it, was still Whore Row in the blocks of the Forties. And Honour Mercy, although she was wearing a sixty-dollar dress, and although her behind did not wiggle when she walked, still half-belonged there. She had not realized this, not consciously, but the men seemed to recognize the fact.

"Girlie!" one of them whispered from a doorway, his eyes hungry. She ignored him and went on walking. Another one mocked with his eyes; his lips curled, and he said. "How much, sister?"

She swept past him.

The one who took her arm was more difficult. But she got rid of him, too, and she kept walking. She walked a block or two more until she was at Eighth and 44th, and here she stopped walking. She stood in front of a drugstore and pretended to interest herself in a display of ancient pharmaceutical instruments, but the mortars and pestles, symbolic of her work as they might be, were not nearly so fascinating as she made out.

Why had she stopped there?

In a vague way, it seemed to her that she might find a friend here, someone to talk to. She was a whore, of course, and Whore

Row seemed the proper place for a whore to look for friends. She certainly didn't want to turn a trick, a cheap ten-buck trick when she had all that money in the bank. So, obviously, she had come to Whore Row to see a friend.

The hell of it was that she didn't have any friends. Not on Whore Row or anyplace else.

But that was silly. She hadn't come there just to stand around like a lamppost. The whole thing didn't make any sense at all.

She turned around slowly, feeling lost and more alone than ever with all of these strangers wandering busily back and forth around her. She told herself that somewhere there was a pattern and it was only a question of discovering it for herself, of locating the pattern and pinning it down and studying it closely.

Whatever it was.

Then there was a woman coming toward her, a woman with frizzy black hair and pale skin and too much makeup on her mouth and cheeks and eyes. At first Honour Mercy looked at her, thought *whore* and looked away. Then she looked again, and this time she recognized the woman and her eyes went wide and her mouth dropped open.

It was Marie.

Marie, the prostitute who had been her first contact in New York. Marie, who had also happened to be a lesbian, the first and last with whom Honour Mercy had come into mildly distasteful contact. When she left Marie she would have been perfectly content not to see the woman ever again, but now, because she was alone and fresh out of patterns, she discovered that she was glad to see her, glad to have the woman take her arm, glad at last to have someone, anyone, to talk to.

"Honey! Well, I'll be damned!"

"Hello," she said. "Hello, Marie."

"Well, I'll be damned!" Marie repeated. Her smile was somehow awkward and her eyes seemed out of focus, a little glassy.

"A long time," Marie was saying. "Little Honey landed on the phone and high-hatted her old friends. Where you been, baby?"

Marie's words were sleepy, coming through a filter. Her eyes were half-closed now and she barely moved her lips when she spoke.

"I've been living uptown," Honour Mercy said. She had to say something.

"Uptown? One of those post pads off the park. That sounds nice. Post pads off the park. All those 'p' sounds. Goes together real nice with a swing to it."

Honour Mercy opened her mouth, then closed it, then opened it again. "You're different," she said.

"Different? Just because I like girls? That's not all that's different, baby. It's my scene. You've got to be tolerant of another person's scene, baby. It's the only way."

"I don't mean that."

"No?"

"Your eyes," Honour Mercy said. "And the way you talk and everything."

Marie giggled. "I didn't know it showed that much. I must be carrying a heavy load."

Honour Mercy didn't understand.

"C'mon out of the light, baby. Around the corner where the bugs don't chase you. Light is evil."

She let Marie take her around the corner to 44th Street. They walked a ways and then the older woman led her into a doorway.

"You tumbled quick," Marie said. "You hipped yourself fast. Or are you making the same scene?"

Honour Mercy was lost. Then Marie lifted her own skirt all the way, and when Honour Mercy's face screwed up in puzzlement she pointed to her legs.

There were marks running up and down the insides of her thighs.

And Honour Mercy understood.

"Junk," Marie said. "H, horse, junk. Sweet little powder that makes happy dreams. You put the needle in and everything gets pretty. You ever make horse? Ever put the needle in and take it out empty?"

"No."

"Ever make pot? Ever break a stick with a buddy? Ever smoke up and dream?"

She shook her head.

"Ever sniff? Ever skin-pop and smile all night at the ceiling?"

"No."

Marie smiled. "A virgin," she said reverently. "A little virgin with bells on. You better let me take your cherry, Honey. Better let Marie turn you on to the world, the pink world. You come with me."

Marie took her arm again, but Honour Mercy stayed where she was.

"Aren't you coming?"

"I don't know."

"You want to come, baby. You want to see what's wrong and what's right. You see the way I am now?"

She nodded.

"High," Marie said. "High in the sky with a pocket full of rye. Four-and-twenty spade birds baking in pie in the sky. Come fly with me."

"I . . . what does it do?"

"Makes the world good," Marie said. "Makes everything fit where it should. Makes a whore a queen. And a cat can look at a queen. Right?"

She hesitated.

"Come *on*," Marie told her. "No charge, no cost. Sample day, every ride a nickel at Coney Island. Ever ride the comet, baby? Or the caterpillar?"

"I—"

"You will, baby. You'll lie down and ride them all, every one of them. This time it'll be you riding instead of some man riding you. You just come on and ride, baby. You just come with me."

Marie had the same room as before. Honour Mercy sat on the edge of the bed, remembering the other time they had been together in Marie's room, remembering what they had done. She wondered what they were going to do now, what it would be like.

Marie was holding a match under a teaspoon. A small white capsule rested in the spoon, and the heat from the match melted it. When it was all liquid, she pushed in the plunger of a hypodermic needle, then sucked up the liquid with it.

"Your leg," Marie said. "Don't want it in your arm or the mark'll show. Want it in your leg, so pull up your dress for me. That's right. And we're not going to turn you on in the vein because you don't need it, not yet. Just a skin-fix, that ought to be enough. Ought to put you up so high you'll fly all over God's little acre. That's right, that's the way."

Marie sank the needle into the fleshy part of Honour Mercy's thigh. Honour Mercy sat, watching the needle go in, watching Marie depress the plunger and send the heroin into her thigh. And she waited for something to happen.

And nothing happened. For a moment or two nothing at all happened and she wanted to tell Marie to stop teasing her.

Then something happened.

And she stretched out on the bed and closed her eyes and stared at heaven through the top of her skull.

CHAPTER 10

It was a big metal room full of women. High on the back wall was a barred window, above the woman-crowded metal bench. That bench, running the full width of the back wall, was the only furniture in the big square metal room. A dozen women sat hip-crowded on the metal bench, dressed in shapeless gray bags of dresses. Another dozen women sat on the scuffed black metal floor. A few more leaned against the gray metal walls, trying to talk. But it was tough to talk, because of the screaming.

Up front, draped against the metal bars like an old newspaper flung there by the wind, Honour Mercy Bane hung screaming. Honey Bane now, Honey Bane now and forever more.

Honey Bane was a mess. Her chestnut hair lay tangled, dull and streaming, stuck to her head like a fright wig. Her face was white, the white of the underbelly of a fish, except for the gray around her staring eyes and the dark red gaping wound of her screaming mouth.

She'd been screaming for a long while, and her voice was getting hoarse. They'd brought her in at three in the morning, two rough-handed cops, and tossed her in the female detention tank with the rest of the dregs scooped from the murky bottom of the city that night, and at first she'd stood hunch-shouldered in a corner, leaning against the wall, chain-smoking and glaring at the hollow-eyed broads who'd tried to talk to her.

At four, she started to pace back and forth across the metal floor and around the perimeter of the walls, pacing and shaking her head and rubbing her upper arms with trembling fingers, as though she were cold. Some of the women, knowing the signs, watched her in silence, like beasts of prey. The rest ignored her.

At five, she began to tremble and stretch and rub her cheeks with hard fingers, and the watching women licked dry lips. At five-fifteen, she fell, rolled, struggled up and lunged into the bars. She hung there, quivering, and at five-twenty-five, she started to scream.

With the first scream, three of the women had darted forward. The first one to reach her jabbed into the pocket of Honey Bane's prison dress and pulled out the crumpled remains of her cigarettes, then ducked away from the angry, envious clutching of the other two. And Honour Mercy screamed for the second time, neither knowing nor caring that her cigarettes had been stolen. It wasn't cigarettes she wanted.

Now it was seven o'clock, and she was still screaming, though her voice was getting hoarse. One or two guards had tried to stop her, telling her the doc would come at seven, but she neither heard nor understood. One or two of the other women, unnerved by the screaming, had tried to stop her, to pull her away from the bars, but she had clung and shrieked and they had given up.

And now it was eight o'clock, and the metal door down at the end of the long gray metal hall clanged open. Two guards came through, followed by an annoyed young man in a business suit. They came down the hall, their shoes ringing on the black metal floor, and the annoyed young man waited while the guards un-locked the detention tank door. The three of them came in, and the guards efficiently peeled Honey Bane from the bars and held her rigid, still screaming, her back against the wall.

The annoyed young man put down his black bag and slapped Honey Bane twice across the face, forehand, backhand. "Stop that," he said, and his voice was emotionless and cold. "I'm going to give you something now."

The silence itself was like a scream, coming so abruptly. Honey Bane blinked rapidly, her eyes tearing, trying to focus on the an-noyed young man. "Give—give—give me—"

"Got to get you ready for the judge," said one of the guards. He grinned, holding her arm with one hand, rolling the gray sleeve up with the other. "Can't have you all shook up in front of the judge," he said.

Honey Bane fought the two realities, the hot hurtful hating reality within, the cold cruel killing reality without, and slowly she forced her attention away from the reality within and saw and heard and smelled and felt the reality without.

She looked upon the real world. In the background, a mob scene from the Inferno, women in shapeless gray, milling and star-ing, scratching their sores, grimacing their lips. In the foreground, the annoyed young man, down on one knee and crouched over his now open black bag, preparing a hypodermic.

A hypodermic. The needle glinted in the light from the un-shaded bulbs high up against the metal ceiling. The needle glint-ed and gleamed, drawing her eyes, drawing her attention, draw-ing her soul.

Her mouth opened, working. "You'll—give—me—something?"

"Sure thing," said the guard. "Got to make you pretty for the judge," he cackled, showing yellowed teeth.

The world was coming back, stronger and stronger. To either side there was a man, holding her. Men in uniform, guards, and the annoyed young man was rising up with the golden gleaming needle, and the one guard had rolled up her right sleeve.

With sudden violence, she shook her head, pulling away, her mouth distorted wide. One thing she knew in all the world, one thing and one thing only, and she screamed it at them. *"Not the arm!"*

"Hold her still," said the annoyed young man. He was petulant, unjustifiably detained, left standing there with the cotton swab in one hand and the golden gleaming needle in the other.

"Not the arm!" shrieked Honey Bane. "The leg, the leg, not the arm!"

The two guards held her, crowded her close against the wall, and the annoyed young man came forward, the cotton swab moving with practiced indifference on her upper arm. "Where you're going," he told her coldly, "it won't make any difference." And the golden gleaming needle jabbed in.

When they let her go, she slumped back, sliding down the wall, her legs crumpled beneath her, her knees sticking up and out, the gray shapeless skirt falling away to her hips. The prison dress was all she was wearing.

The two guards looked at her, grinning, but the annoyed young man curled his lip and pointedly looked the other way. The guards unlocked the tank door, and they and the annoyed young man stepped through to the hall. The door was relocked, and three men walked back down the echoing hall and through the door at the far end.

Now that there was silence, more of the women got into conversations, and some of them lay down on the floor to try to get a little sleep before appearing in court. A few of them, new and curious and uncertain, watched Honey Bane with wondering eyes.

But she didn't notice the looks or hear the conversations or know that her skirt was piled high about her hips. The outside reality had faded away once again, and the reality within had taken over. Slowly, quiveringly, painfully, far down within the crumpled huddled body that was and wasn't Honey Bane, she was beginning to live again. Slowly, she was being reborn, she was returning from the dead. High hot color began to glow in her face. Her hands, which had been trembling and shaking so badly just a few moments before, grew still and languid. Her whole body relaxed, as tension drained away, leaving her limp and unmoving. Her eyes were distant and high-seeing, gleaming with a pale life of their own.

She stood, with slow and languid movements, and waited unmoving, her arms hanging still at her sides, her eyes almost blank-looking, staring far off at the reality within.

She had returned from the dead. On the island of Haiti, they would have called her undead, the zombie. On Manhattan Island, where the magic phrases were different, they called her junkie, the snowbird.

It took a while for the first high keening to wear off, and for Honey Bane to gradually circle down from that high-flying cloud and descend close enough to make out the details of the reality without. Finally, though, she did come down, and saw and realized where she was.

And this time, she realized, they'd picked her up just before she was due for a needle. And she was carrying the stuff on her when she'd been grabbed. So now they had her on a user rap.

That was bad—very bad. A simple charge of soliciting wasn't anything to worry about all by itself—she'd been through that she didn't know how many times, and she'd never gotten more than a suspended sentence out of it for disorderly behavior—but a user rap was something else again. It would mean six months at Lexington, taking the cure. It would mean getting dragged in by the cops every time there was a general narcotics pick-up. It would mean having cops banging on the door all the time, breaking in and looking for more of the stuff.

That's the way it had been with Marie. Twice she'd been grabbed and convicted on user raps. The first time, she got the six-month taper-off cure at Lexington. The second time, she got the cold-turkey cure at a state hospital out on Long Island.

The third time they hadn't wasted time with a user charge. She'd taken a fall for possession, and was now in the woman's prison upstate, on a seven-to-ten. And Marie wasn't the type to get time off for good behavior. Whatever years she had left when she could make a dime hustling, she'd be spending behind bars. By the time she got out, she'd be through. Too old to make it on Whore Row; too beat up to make it anywhere else. And she'd be back on the big H in forty-eight hours, with no way to raise the cash to feed the monkey on her back.

That was no way to go. Honey Bane was now starting down the same three steps Marie had taken, and she knew she couldn't afford to go down more than just the first step. She'd have to make sure she fell no further.

It never occurred to her to keep away from the stuff once she'd had the cure and been freed. No, that wasn't a solution, not conceivably a solution. She would simply have to be more careful in the future, that was all. She'd have to find some absolutely safe hiding place for the stuff.

There was Roxanne. Since Marie had been sent up on the possession charge, Honey had found herself a new lover. Roxanne, a young kid from South Dakota somewhere, a short, fiery brunette, now working Whore Row. Roxanne wasn't a user, and she'd never even been pulled in by the cops on a soliciting charge. Her place would be as safe as a convent. The stuff could be left there, and Honey could stop by every time she needed a fix. That would work out, all right, that would work out fine.

As for Lexington, there was nothing to worry about there. As a matter of fact, it would be a nice little vacation. No hustling, no crazy hours or eating greasy meals in Eighth Avenue luncheonettes, no dodging the cops all the time.

And the best part of it was that they believed in the slow cure at Lexington. That meant she'd be getting free H for the next few months, and that was heaven. The amount would gradually taper off, and eventually they'd stop feeding it to her completely, but that was way off in the future somewhere, and she didn't have to worry about it. Free H. It was the goddam answer to a maiden's prayer that's what it was.

And when she came back, she'd stash the stuff with Roxanne. No problems.

One problem, maybe. Roxanne was young, damn

good-looking. She was just liable to get switched to the phone business. That would be a good break for her, of course; she'd make damn good money, have a nice apartment uptown and go out with the better class of customers. But it would also mean the end of her relationship with Honey Bane. Honey knew how that worked. She'd been on the phone herself, and she knew that the girls who worked the phone didn't hang around with the girls who worked the street.

She nodded, smiling to herself, lost in her memories. She'd been on the phone herself, she had, and she'd had a great little apartment uptown. Until that one lousy customer had seen the marks on the insides of her legs and bitched that he hadn't paid to get mixed up with a junkie. Then all of a sudden she hadn't been working the phone anymore. She'd been back to working the street.

But maybe it wouldn't happen. Maybe Marie—no, Roxanne—maybe Roxanne wouldn't get switched over to the phone. There was no sense worrying about it, anyway. No sense worrying about anything.

At eight o'clock, a matron came, a stocky, sour-faced woman in an unattractive uniform, and took Honey Bane away, holding her with a too-tight grip on the elbow. Honey went willingly, not worrying about anything, not caring about anything, and the matron led her to a small room where her clothes were waiting, and she changed from the prison dress back to her own clothes, and the matron turned her over to a guard to be taken up to the court.

The courtroom was up on the next floor. The guard led the way to the stairwell, and stood aside for Honey to go first up the stairs. She did so, and the guard slid his hand up her leg, beneath the skirt, grabbing her.

Her voice flat, she said, "I hope you get syphilis of the hand."

He jerked his hand away, and growled, "You're a tough one, huh?"

She didn't bother to answer.

He reached up and grasped her elbow, pinching it with his fingers, saying, "Not so fast, girlie. There's no rush."

She allowed herself to be led up the rest of the way and into the courtroom. Then she had to wait for fifteen minutes, sitting in the front row while the judge worked with people ahead of her.

This was Judge McBee. He smiled and told jokes, and called the defendants by their first names. He could skin you, slowly, with a hot knife, but he'd smile and joke and make friendly chatter all the while. Everybody along Whore Row knew Judge McBee. They hated his guts.

She sat, not listening, not caring, in a soft and pleasant haze. After the first hard jolt and the crystal clarity of thought, she had sunk slowly into a soft cottony mist, and she would be there now for most of the day. She sat, not listening, not thinking about where she was or what was happening to her, and they had to call her name twice before she realized it was her turn before the bar of justice.

She got to her feet, and a guard walked her forward, placed her in front of the judge's high bench. She looked up at him, the round cheerful face framed with gray-white hair, and he beamed down at her, nodding and saying, "Well, now, Honey, I thought I wasn't going to be seeing you anymore."

She smiled a little in return. "Me, too," she said.

"Looks like things are a lot more serious this time," said the judge happily. He pawed among the official documents on his desk, and the young man to his right reached over his shoulder and plucked out the particular paper he wanted. The young man was Edward McBee, the judge's nephew, a law student up in Connecticut. He'd asked Judge McBee to let him sit in at court, behind the judge's bench, to see the proceedings from the judge's angle of vision.

Judge McBee now took the paper from his nephew, beaming and nodding his thanks, and slowly read the document. Finished at last, he peered at Honey Bane and said, "It says here you were found with heroin on your person, Honey. You using that stuff now?"

"Yes," she said.

Edward McBee strained forward, his eager face inches from his uncle's black-clothed shoulder, and stared at Honey Bane, as though trying to see Honour Mercy, lurking somewhere far beneath.

"That's terrible stuff, Honey," said the judge. "You want to get off that, you hear me?"

Some answer was expected of her. She felt a moment of panic, until she realized she could answer the last part of the question. Yes, she did hear him. "Yes," she said.

"Now," said Judge McBee, "I'm going to have you sent to Lexington. Have you heard of Lexington?"

"That's where they have the slow cure," she said.

"That's right." He beamed paternally at her, pleased with the right answer. "I'll have you sent there, for six months. And when you come back, I want you to stay away from narcotics.

Completely." He looked down at his papers again, and smiled suddenly. "I'm going to help you, Honey," he said. "I'm going to help you stay away from narcotics. You have also been charged with disorderly conduct, you know. Soliciting again. The last time you were here, you promised me you wouldn't be doing that anymore."

She hung her head, hating him. There was nothing she could say.

"When you come back, then," he said cheerfully, "you can begin a ninety-day sentence in the city jail for disorderly conduct. That's to begin the day you are released from Lexington." Uncapping a silver fountain pen, he wrote hastily, and looked up once again, smiling. "I won't be seeing you for a while, Honey," he said. "Not for nine months. You be a good girl in Lexington, now."

"Yes," she said.

"And I'll see you in nine months."

"Yes."

He shook his head, smiling sadly. "Yes," he said. "I'll see you here again in nine months. You won't be changing, will you? All right, Honey, that's all. Go on with the matron."

Another hand was gripping Honey Bane's elbow, too hard, and she let herself be taken away, through the door to the left of the judge's bench, as Edward McBee stared after her, his forehead creased in the lines of a puzzled frown.

Nine months. She hated that bastard. In nine months, Roxanne would be God knew where. She'd have to find somebody else to hold the stuff.

•       •       •

Court was finished for the day, and Judge McBee sat with his nephew in his office, smoking his first cigarette of the day. "Well, Edward," he said. "How did it look from my side of the bench?"

"Frightening," said Edward McBee earnestly. "Sitting back in the spectator's seats, you don't see the expressions on their faces. That girl—"

Judge McBee raised a humorous eyebrow. "Girl?"

"The one you called Honey. Charged with using heroin."

"Oh, yes." Judge McBee nodded, smiling. "She's an old friend," he said. "In once or twice a month, for playing the prostitute. Been around for years."

"How old is she?"

"Oh, I don't know. Twenty-four, I suppose, maybe twenty-five."

"She looked thirty or more."

"They get that look," said the judge wisely. "It's the kind of life they lead."

"How does a girl like that get involved in such a life?" his nephew asked him.

"A girl like what?"

The nephew blinked in embarrassment at his uncle's amusement. "There was something about that girl—" He stopped in confusion.

"Now don't go romanticizing a common whore," said the judge sternly. "That's all the girl is, a common whore."

"But how did she get that way, that's what I want know. How did she get that way?"

"They're *born* that way," the judge told him. "It's simple as that. They're born that way, and nothing can change them." He heaved to his feet. "Now, let's get some lunch," he said. "I'm starving."

**My Newsletter:** I get out an email newsletter at unpredictable intervals, but rarely more often than every other week. I'll be happy to add you to the distribution list. A blank email to lawbloc@gmail.com with "newsletter" in the subject line will get you on the list, and a click of the "Unsubscribe" link will get you off it, should you ultimately decide you're happier without it.

**Lawrence Block** has been writing award-winning mystery and suspense fiction for half a century. You can read his thoughts about crime fiction and crime writers in *The Crime of Our Lives*, where this MWA Grand Master tells it straight. His most recent novels are *The Girl With the Deep Blue Eyes*; *The Burglar Who Counted the Spoons*, featuring Bernie Rhodenbarr; *Hit Me*, featuring Keller; and *A Drop of the Hard Stuff*, featuring Matthew Scudder, played by Liam Neeson in the film *A Walk Among the Tombstones*. Several of his other books have been filmed, although not terribly well. He's well known for his books for writers, including the classic *Telling Lies for Fun &f Profit*, and *The Liar's Bible*. In addition to prose works, he has written episodic television (*Tilt!*) and the Wong Kar-wai film, *My Blueberry Nights*. He is a modest and humble fellow, although you would never guess as much from this biographical note.

Email: lawbloc@gmail.com
Twitter: @LawrenceBlock
Facebook: lawrence.block
Website: lawrenceblock.com